# TRIAL OF THE AMAZONS

DEC - 2022

VITA AYALA, BECKY CLOONAN, MICHAEL W. CONRAD,
JOËLLE JONES, STEPHANIE WILLIAMS, JORDIE BELLAIRE writers

LAURA BRAGA, ELENA CASAGRANDE, BECKY CLOONAN, JOËLLE JONES, ROSI KÄMPE, PAULINA GANUCHEAU, ALITHA MARTINEZ, ADRIANA MELO, MARK MORALES, SKYLAR PATRIDGE artists

# TRIAL OF THE AMAZONS

JORDIE BELLAIRE, TAMRA BONVILLAIN, KENDALL GOODE, ROMULO FAJARDO JR., MARISSA LOUISE colorists

PAT BROSSEAU, BECCA CAREY letterers

JIM CHEUNG and JAY DAVID RAMOS collection cover artists

Wonder Woman created by William Moulton Marston

TRIAL OF THE AMAZONS



DC Comics, 100 S. California Street, Burbank, CA 91505
Printed by Transcontinental Interglobe, Beauceville, QC, Canada. 8/26/22. First Printing.
ISBN: 978-1-77951-682-4

Library of Congress Cataloging-in-Publication Data is available.

PEFC Certified
This product is from sustainably managed forests and controlled sources
PEFC
PEFC/01-31-106
www.pefc.org

THEMYSCIRA. YEARS AGO.
I FEEL MORE COMFORTABLE ALL THE TIME WITH THE IDEA OF BEING QUEEN SOMEDAY.
I AM ALWAYS LEARNING FROM MY SISTERS.
I'M BECOMING CERTAIN THAT I KNOW WHAT MAKES A GREAT LEADER...

WHAM
DIANA! GOOD MORNING, LIGHT OF MY LIFE. TIME TO RISE AND SHINE!
...BUT THERE'S ALWAYS MORE TO LEARN.
WHAT IS IT, DID I SCARE YOU?
I AM FOREVER CHILLED. THANK YOU, MOTHER.
OH, WELL, I HAVE JUST THE THING FOR YOU! TODAY YOU'RE IN FOR VERY RIGOROUS AND INTENSIVE LEADERSHIP LESSONS FROM YOUR FAVORITE TEACHER!
CLIO?
ME, DIANA. YOUR MOTHER! DON'T MAKE ME BANISH CLIO FROM THEMYSCIRA.
I JEST! REALLY THOUGH, PLEASE DRESS APPROPRIATELY FOR SUCH A HARD DAY'S WORK!
EXTRA FOLDS IN THE ROBES, GOT IT.

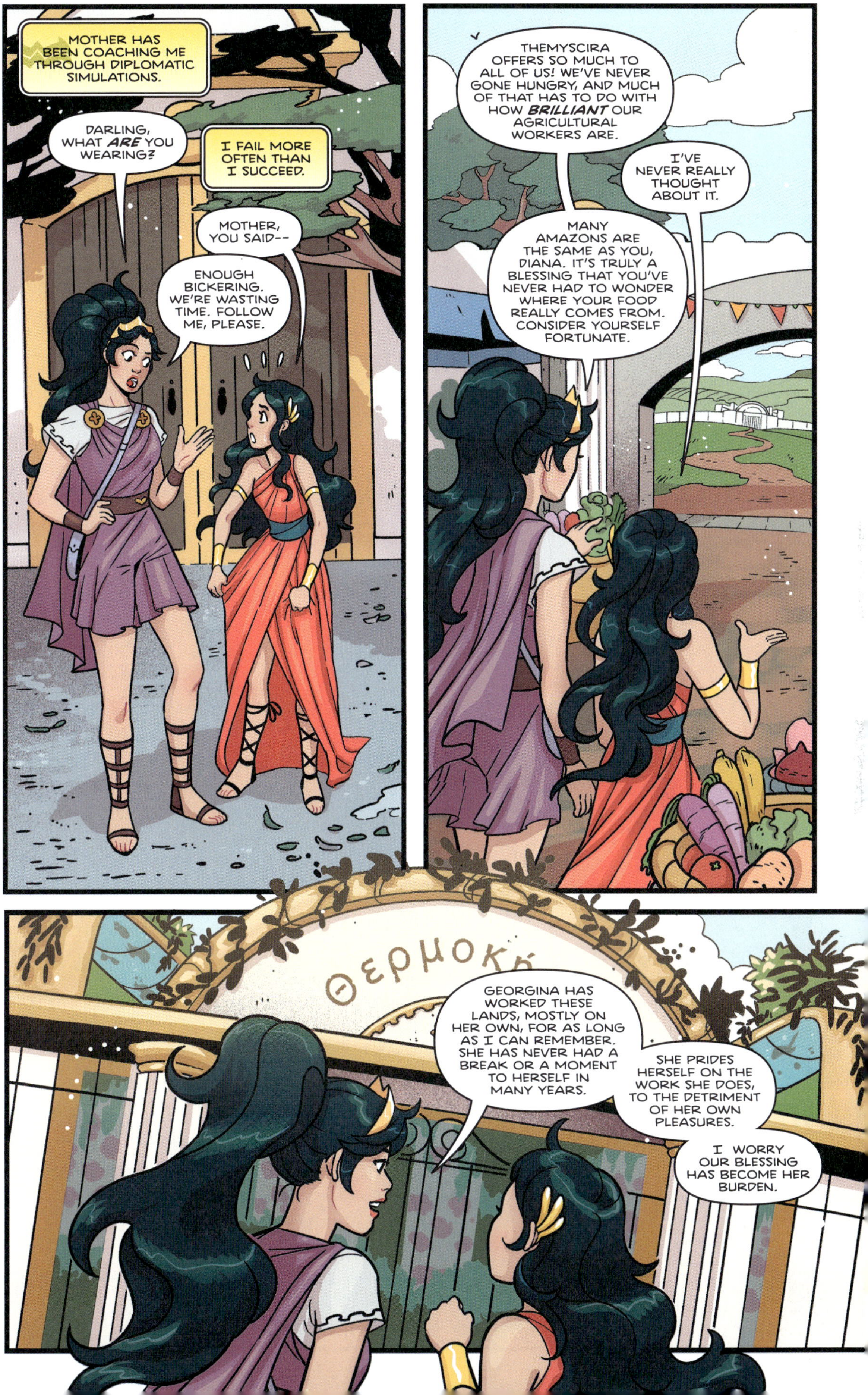
MOTHER HAS BEEN COACHING ME THROUGH DIPLOMATIC SIMULATIONS.
DARLING, WHAT ARE YOU WEARING?
I FAIL MORE OFTEN THAN I SUCCEED.
MOTHER, YOU SAID--
ENOUGH BICKERING. WE'RE WASTING TIME. FOLLOW ME, PLEASE.
THEMYSCIRA OFFERS SO MUCH TO ALL OF US! WE'VE NEVER GONE HUNGRY, AND MUCH OF THAT HAS TO DO WITH HOW BRILLIANT OUR AGRICULTURAL WORKERS ARE.
I'VE NEVER REALLY THOUGHT ABOUT IT.
MANY AMAZONS ARE THE SAME AS YOU, DIANA. IT'S TRULY A BLESSING THAT YOU'VE NEVER HAD TO WONDER WHERE YOUR FOOD REALLY COMES FROM. CONSIDER YOURSELF FORTUNATE.
ΘΕΡΜΟΚ
GEORGINA HAS WORKED THESE LANDS, MOSTLY ON HER OWN, FOR AS LONG AS I CAN REMEMBER. SHE HAS NEVER HAD A BREAK OR A MOMENT TO HERSELF IN MANY YEARS.
SHE PRIDES HERSELF ON THE WORK SHE DOES, TO THE DETRIMENT OF HER OWN PLEASURES.
I WORRY OUR BLESSING HAS BECOME HER BURDEN.

WOW.
IT'S LIKE ANOTHER WORLD, ISN'T IT?
THEMYSCIRA ALWAYS SEEMS TO SURPRISE ME.
HIPPOLYTA! I TOLD YOU, I WON'T BE TAKING ANY TIME OFF!
GEORGINA! HELLO!

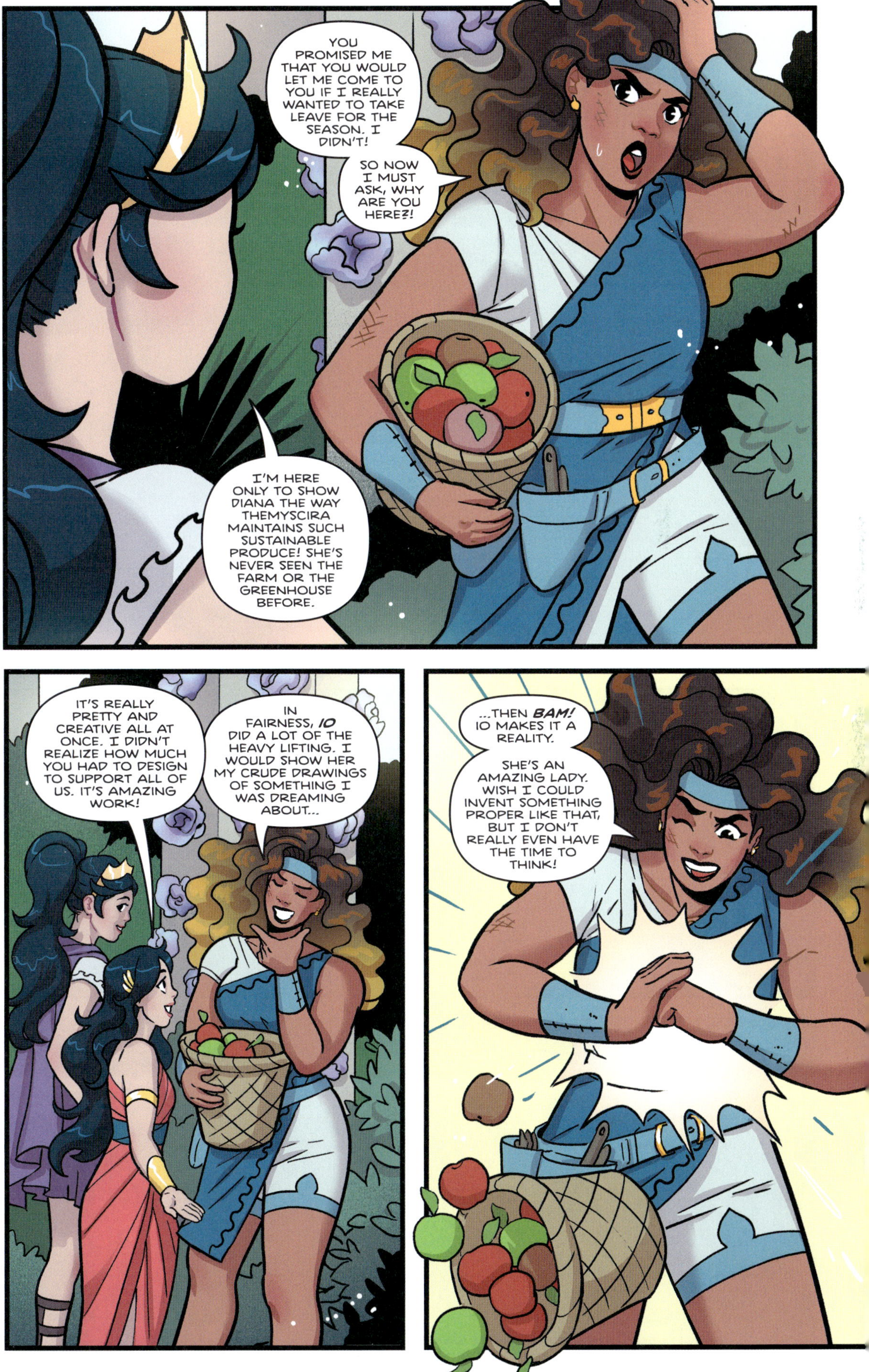
YOU PROMISED ME THAT YOU WOULD LET ME COME TO YOU IF I REALLY WANTED TO TAKE LEAVE FOR THE SEASON. I DIDN'T!
SO NOW I MUST ASK, WHY ARE YOU HERE?!
I'M HERE ONLY TO SHOW DIANA THE WAY THEMYSCIRA MAINTAINS SUCH SUSTAINABLE PRODUCE! SHE'S NEVER SEEN THE FARM OR THE GREENHOUSE BEFORE.
IT'S REALLY PRETTY AND CREATIVE ALL AT ONCE. I DIDN'T REALIZE HOW MUCH YOU HAD TO DESIGN TO SUPPORT ALL OF US. IT'S AMAZING WORK!
IN FAIRNESS, ***IO*** DID A LOT OF THE HEAVY LIFTING. I WOULD SHOW HER MY CRUDE DRAWINGS OF SOMETHING I WAS DREAMING ABOUT...
...THEN ***BAM!*** IO MAKES IT A REALITY.
SHE'S AN AMAZING LADY. WISH I COULD INVENT SOMETHING PROPER LIKE THAT, BUT I DON'T REALLY EVEN HAVE THE TIME TO THINK!

SURE, IT WOULD BE NICE TO TRADE PLACES WITH SOMEONE LIKE THAT--A LOT OF IT COMES DOWN TO WHAT YOU'RE BORN WITH, RIGHT, MOTHER?
THIS IS TRUE, DIANA! GEORGINA HAS A *BEAUTIFUL* GREEN THUMB!
IT'S TRUE, LOOK AT IT!
IT DOESN'T LOOK VERY GREEN TO ME?
YOU PUT HER UP TO THAT, HIPPOLYTA?
WHY WOULD I EVER DO A THING LIKE THAT? I'M SO VERY GRATEFUL FOR YOUR AGRICULTURAL PROWESS.
*OKAY,* IT'S BEEN FUN BUT WE'VE GOT WORK TO DO HERE. THE SUN IS ONLY OUT SO MANY HOURS AND WE'VE GOT A LOT TO DO BEFORE THE HARVEST. I'M ALREADY STRESSED TO THE GILLS WITH THE FESTIVAL YOU'VE GOT PLANNED IN A FEW WEEKS, TIME, SO IT'S BEST YOU GET GOING.
GO ON NOW. SHOO.

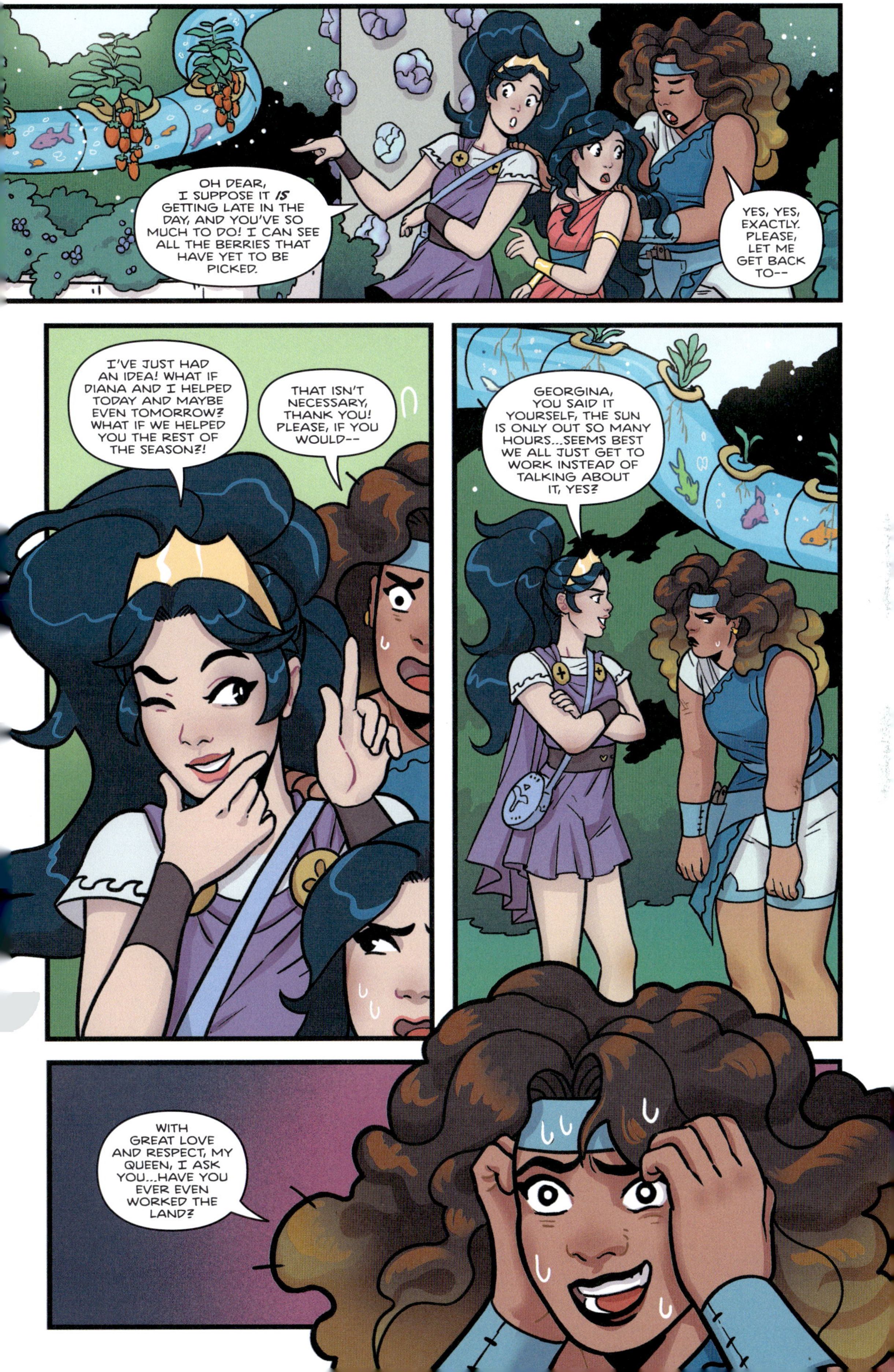
OH DEAR, I SUPPOSE IT IS GETTING LATE IN THE DAY, AND YOU'VE SO MUCH TO DO! I CAN SEE ALL THE BERRIES THAT HAVE YET TO BE PICKED.
YES, YES, EXACTLY. PLEASE, LET ME GET BACK TO--
I'VE JUST HAD AN IDEA! WHAT IF DIANA AND I HELPED TODAY AND MAYBE EVEN TOMORROW? WHAT IF WE HELPED YOU THE REST OF THE SEASON?!
THAT ISN'T NECESSARY, THANK YOU! PLEASE, IF YOU WOULD--
GEORGINA, YOU SAID IT YOURSELF, THE SUN IS ONLY OUT SO MANY HOURS...SEEMS BEST WE ALL JUST GET TO WORK INSTEAD OF TALKING ABOUT IT, YES?
WITH GREAT LOVE AND RESPECT, MY QUEEN, I ASK YOU...HAVE YOU EVER EVEN WORKED THE LAND?

NO... BUT IT WON'T STOP ME FROM TRYING!
DIANA, BE A DEAR AND FETCH ME THAT SPADE!
UH, YES, MOTHER!
ATHENA, WHAT HAVE I DONE TO DESERVE THIS?
MY MOTHER, LIKE THEMYSCIRA, IS FULL OF SURPRISES TOO.
DC COMICS PROUDLY PRESENTS
YOUNG DIANA IN
MAKE HAY WHILE THE SUN SHINES
WRITER JORDIE BELLAIRE
ART PAULINA GANUCHEAU
COLORS KENDALL GOODE
LETTERS BECCA CAREY
ASSOCIATE EDITOR CHRIS ROSA
EDITOR BRITTANY HOLZHERR
SENIOR EDITOR PAUL KAMINSKI
WONDER WOMAN CREATED BY WILLIAM MOULTON MARSTON

THE GARDENS OF THEMYSCIRA.
OH, WHOOPS! IS THIS EASY TO REPLACE?
I'VE BEEN CULTIVATING THAT PLANT FOR THE BETTER PART OF A CENTURY...
FWUP
IS IT POSSIBLE TO EVER REALLY KNOW YOUR MOTHER?
HIPPOLYTA! WATCH WHERE YOU'RE--
OH DEAR, I'M SO CLUMSY!
I SAY THAT AS SOMEONE WHO UNCOVERED HER DARKEST SECRETS...
WAIT, THE WIND! YOU SHOULD THROW LOWER AND--
SURELY WE'LL HAVE THIS BEAUTIFUL CROP THROUGHOUT THEMYSCIRA...
WHOOSH
OH, THE SEA GOBBLED IT UP, GEORGINA.
...I JUST NEVER KNOW WHAT THIS WOMAN IS THINKING.

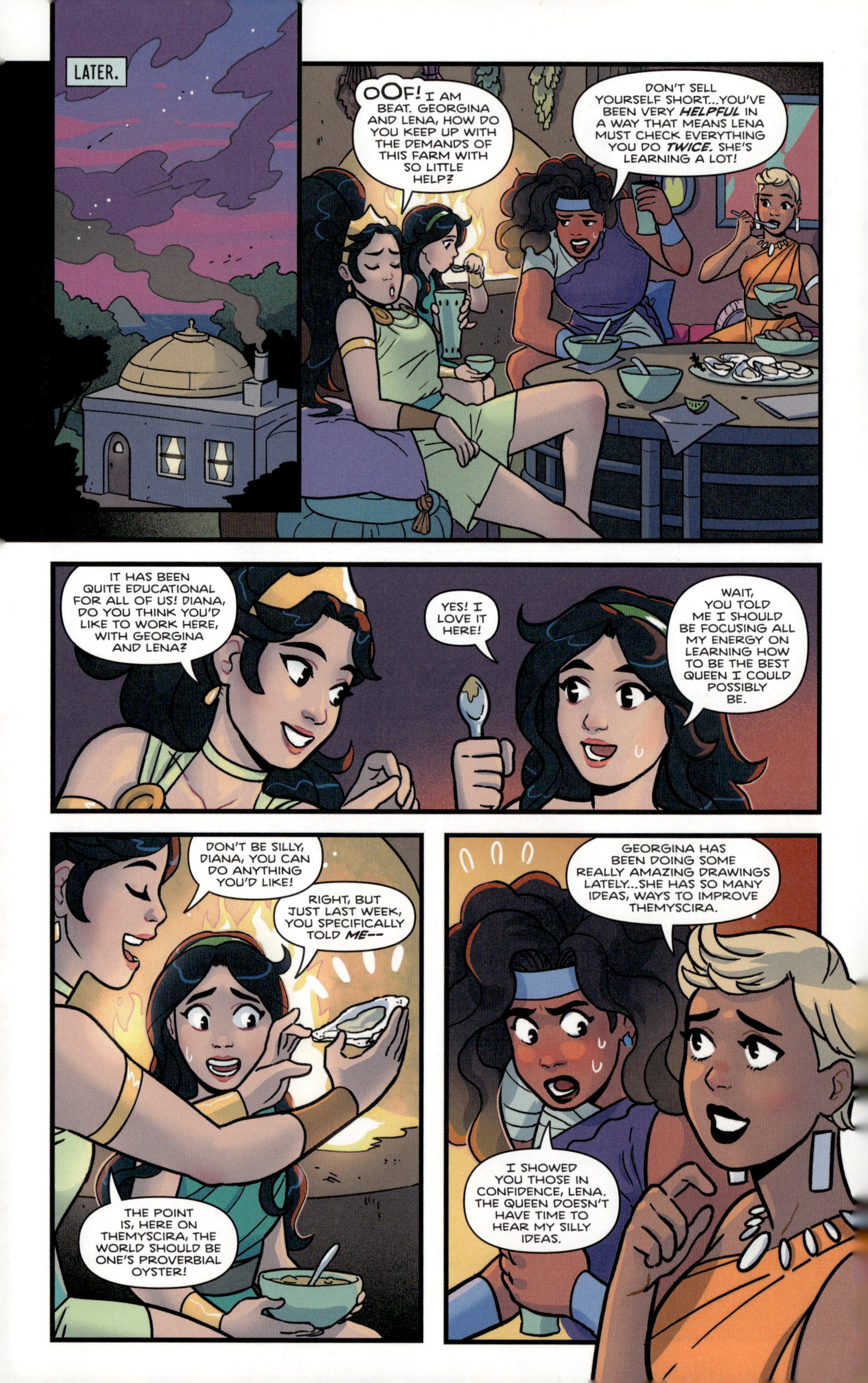
LATER.
OOF! I AM BEAT. GEORGINA AND LENA, HOW DO YOU KEEP UP WITH THE DEMANDS OF THIS FARM WITH SO LITTLE HELP?
DON'T SELL YOURSELF SHORT...YOU'VE BEEN VERY HELPFUL IN A WAY THAT MEANS LENA MUST CHECK EVERYTHING YOU DO TWICE. SHE'S LEARNING A LOT!
IT HAS BEEN QUITE EDUCATIONAL FOR ALL OF US! DIANA, DO YOU THINK YOU'D LIKE TO WORK HERE, WITH GEORGINA AND LENA?
YES! I LOVE IT HERE!
WAIT, YOU TOLD ME I SHOULD BE FOCUSING ALL MY ENERGY ON LEARNING HOW TO BE THE BEST QUEEN I COULD POSSIBLY BE.
DON'T BE SILLY, DIANA, YOU CAN DO ANYTHING YOU'D LIKE!
RIGHT, BUT JUST LAST WEEK, YOU SPECIFICALLY TOLD ME--
THE POINT IS, HERE ON THEMYSCIRA, THE WORLD SHOULD BE ONE'S PROVERBIAL OYSTER!
GEORGINA HAS BEEN DOING SOME REALLY AMAZING DRAWINGS LATELY...SHE HAS SO MANY IDEAS, WAYS TO IMPROVE THEMYSCIRA.
I SHOWED YOU THOSE IN CONFIDENCE, LENA. THE QUEEN DOESN'T HAVE TIME TO HEAR MY SILLY IDEAS.

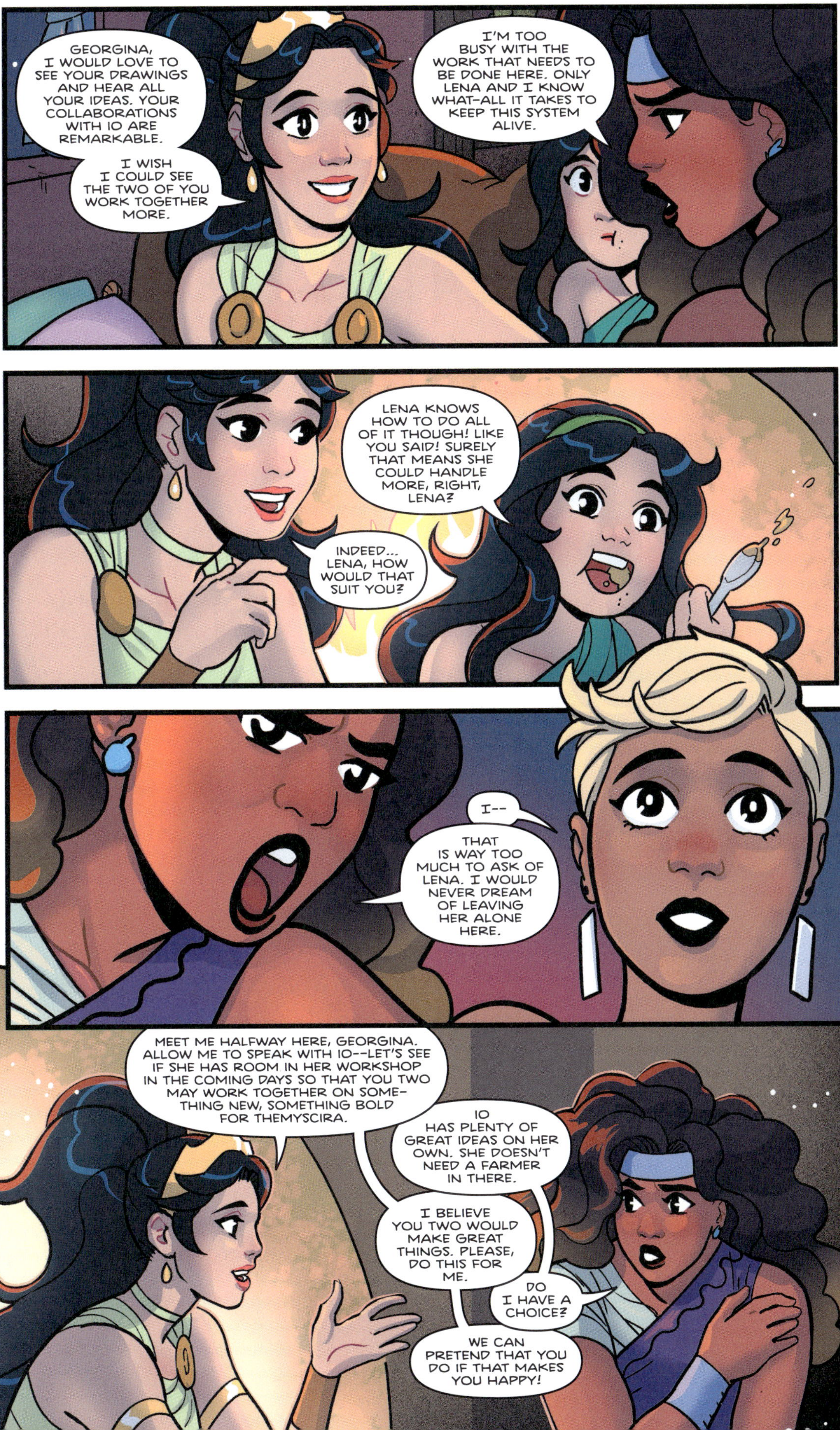
GEORGINA, I WOULD LOVE TO SEE YOUR DRAWINGS AND HEAR ALL YOUR IDEAS. YOUR COLLABORATIONS WITH IO ARE REMARKABLE.
I WISH I COULD SEE THE TWO OF YOU WORK TOGETHER MORE.
I'M TOO BUSY WITH THE WORK THAT NEEDS TO BE DONE HERE. ONLY LENA AND I KNOW WHAT-ALL IT TAKES TO KEEP THIS SYSTEM ALIVE.
LENA KNOWS HOW TO DO ALL OF IT THOUGH! LIKE YOU SAID! SURELY THAT MEANS SHE COULD HANDLE MORE, RIGHT, LENA?
INDEED... LENA, HOW WOULD THAT SUIT YOU?
I--
THAT IS WAY TOO MUCH TO ASK OF LENA. I WOULD NEVER DREAM OF LEAVING HER ALONE HERE.
MEET ME HALFWAY HERE, GEORGINA. ALLOW ME TO SPEAK WITH IO--LET'S SEE IF SHE HAS ROOM IN HER WORKSHOP IN THE COMING DAYS SO THAT YOU TWO MAY WORK TOGETHER ON SOMETHING NEW, SOMETHING BOLD FOR THEMYSCIRA.
IO HAS PLENTY OF GREAT IDEAS ON HER OWN. SHE DOESN'T NEED A FARMER IN THERE.
I BELIEVE YOU TWO WOULD MAKE GREAT THINGS. PLEASE, DO THIS FOR ME.
DO I HAVE A CHOICE?
WE CAN PRETEND THAT YOU DO IF THAT MAKES YOU HAPPY!

THE NEXT DAY.
IT'S IMPORTANT TO ALWAYS CHECK THE WIND BEFORE YOU THROW. I LIKE TO GET REAL LOW TO MAKE SURE I SEE WHERE THEY LAND. I THINK OF THE SEEDS AS HUNDREDS OF LITTLE FRIENDS I HAVEN'T MET YET.
CAN I TRY?
SURE!
THE FISH HELP OUR PRODUCE BECOME BIG AND STRONG!
WOW! HOW DO THE FISH SURVIVE IN THERE?
THE PLANTS KEEP THE WATER EXTRA CLEAR AND CLEAN FOR THE FISH AND WE FEED THEM REGULARLY!
GEORGINA WAS UPSET THAT HIPPOLYTA HARVESTED THIS A LITTLE TOO EARLY, BUT I FIND THE ROOTS GO GREAT WITH STEW. THEY ARE EXTRA SAVORY!
YOU CAN COOK TOO?!
SURE! NOTHING BETTER THAN GROWING WHAT YOU EAT. FROM THE FARM TO OUR BELLIES!
WHAT A WONDERFUL DAY. THANK YOU, LENA.
YES, THANK YOU, LENA!

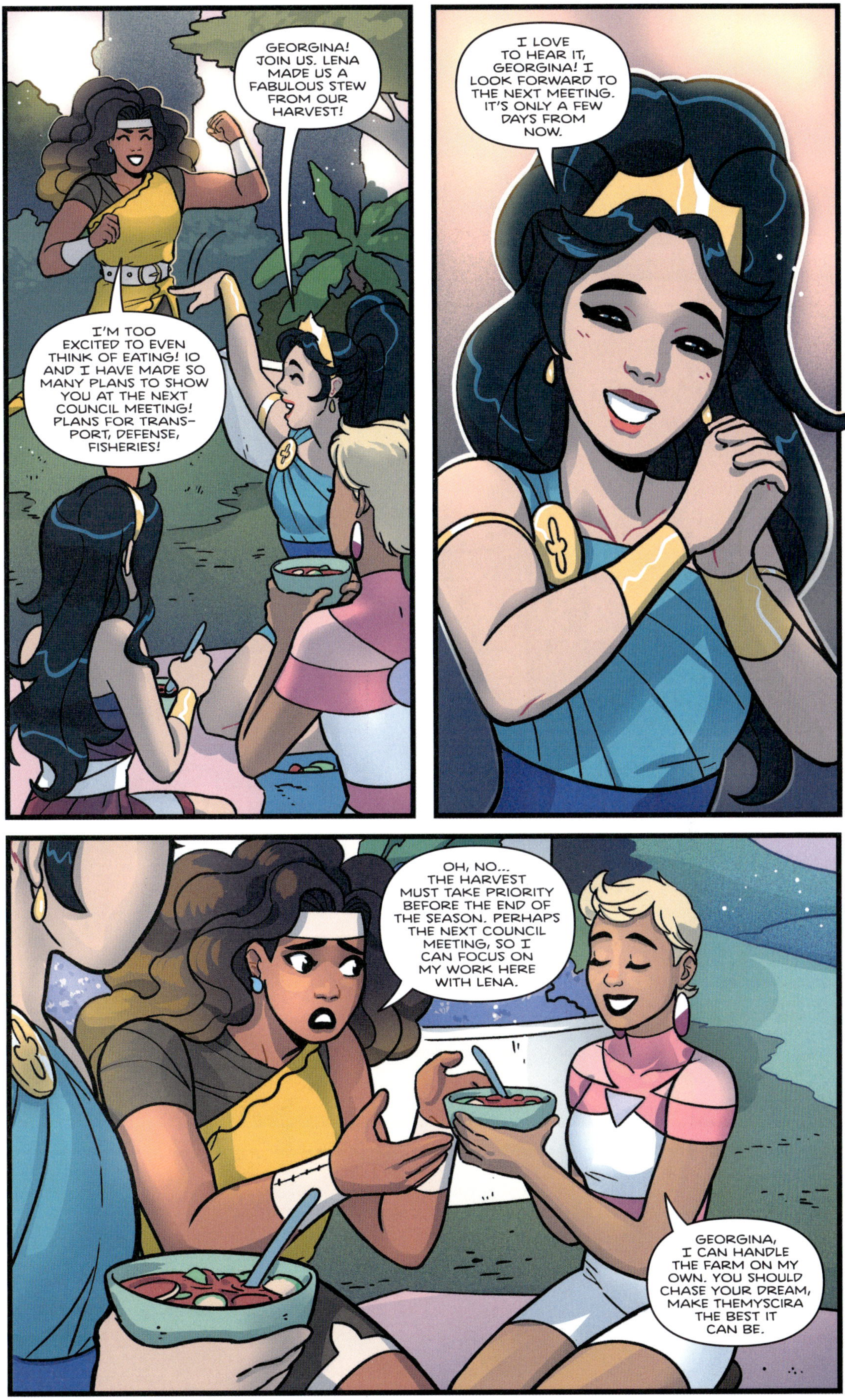
GEORGINA! JOIN US. LENA MADE US A FABULOUS STEW FROM OUR HARVEST!
I'M TOO EXCITED TO EVEN THINK OF EATING! IO AND I HAVE MADE SO MANY PLANS TO SHOW YOU AT THE NEXT COUNCIL MEETING! PLANS FOR TRANS-PORT, DEFENSE, FISHERIES!
I LOVE TO HEAR IT, GEORGINA! I LOOK FORWARD TO THE NEXT MEETING. IT'S ONLY A FEW DAYS FROM NOW.
OH, NO... THE HARVEST MUST TAKE PRIORITY BEFORE THE END OF THE SEASON. PERHAPS THE NEXT COUNCIL MEETING, SO I CAN FOCUS ON MY WORK HERE WITH LENA.
GEORGINA, I CAN HANDLE THE FARM ON MY OWN. YOU SHOULD CHASE YOUR DREAM, MAKE THEMYSCIRA THE BEST IT CAN BE.

BUT...I'M THEMYSCIRA'S FARMER. I...MUST DO WHAT I WAS CHOSEN TO DO.
I DON'T RECALL ANYTHING BEING SET IN STONE. AND EVEN IF IT WERE, THIS IS EXACTLY WHY THE GODS CREATED HAMMERS.
LENA... ARE YOU SURE? THERE IS SO MUCH TO DO AND YOU'RE THE ONLY PERSON HERE MUCH OF THE TIME.
I'VE GOT THIS. I LEARNED EVERYTHING FROM YOU.
YOU'VE GIVEN ME A GIFT. I CAN FINALLY SHARE MORE OF *MYSELF* WITH OUR SISTERS.
YOU'VE GIVEN ME JUST AS MUCH AS I'VE GIVEN YOU. THANK YOU FOR TRUSTING ME WITH ALL THAT YOU'VE BUILT.
HAS MY MOTHER ALWAYS BEEN SO CALCULATING?

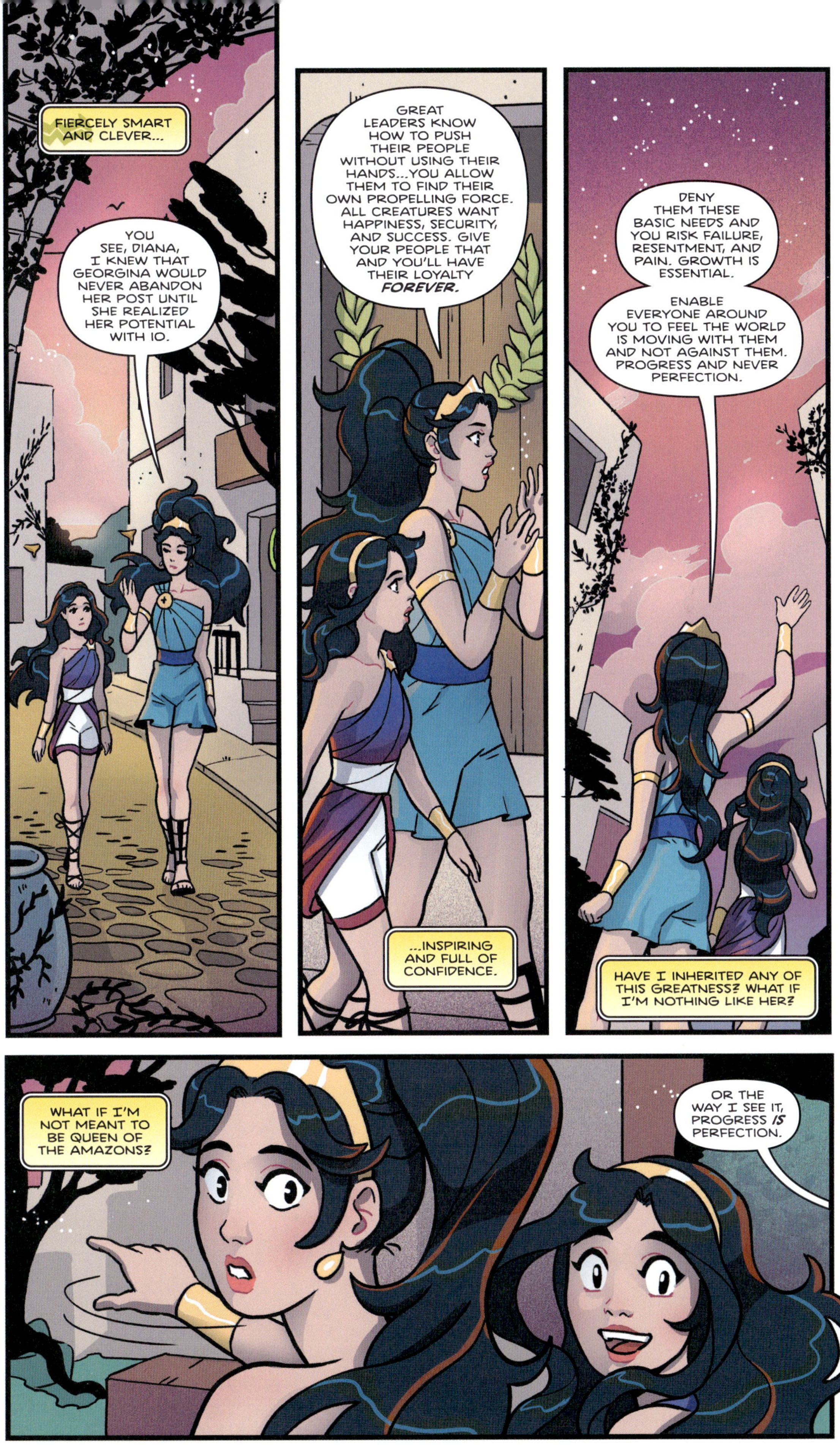
FIERCELY SMART AND CLEVER...
YOU SEE, DIANA, I KNEW THAT GEORGINA WOULD NEVER ABANDON HER POST UNTIL SHE REALIZED HER POTENTIAL WITH IO.
GREAT LEADERS KNOW HOW TO PUSH THEIR PEOPLE WITHOUT USING THEIR HANDS...YOU ALLOW THEM TO FIND THEIR OWN PROPELLING FORCE. ALL CREATURES WANT HAPPINESS, SECURITY, AND SUCCESS. GIVE YOUR PEOPLE THAT AND YOU'LL HAVE THEIR LOYALTY *FOREVER.*
...INSPIRING AND FULL OF CONFIDENCE.
DENY THEM THESE BASIC NEEDS AND YOU RISK FAILURE, RESENTMENT, AND PAIN. GROWTH IS ESSENTIAL.
ENABLE EVERYONE AROUND YOU TO FEEL THE WORLD IS MOVING WITH THEM AND NOT AGAINST THEM. PROGRESS AND NEVER PERFECTION.
HAVE I INHERITED ANY OF THIS GREATNESS? WHAT IF I'M NOTHING LIKE HER?
WHAT IF I'M NOT MEANT TO BE QUEEN OF THE AMAZONS?
OR THE WAY I SEE IT, PROGRESS *IS* PERFECTION.

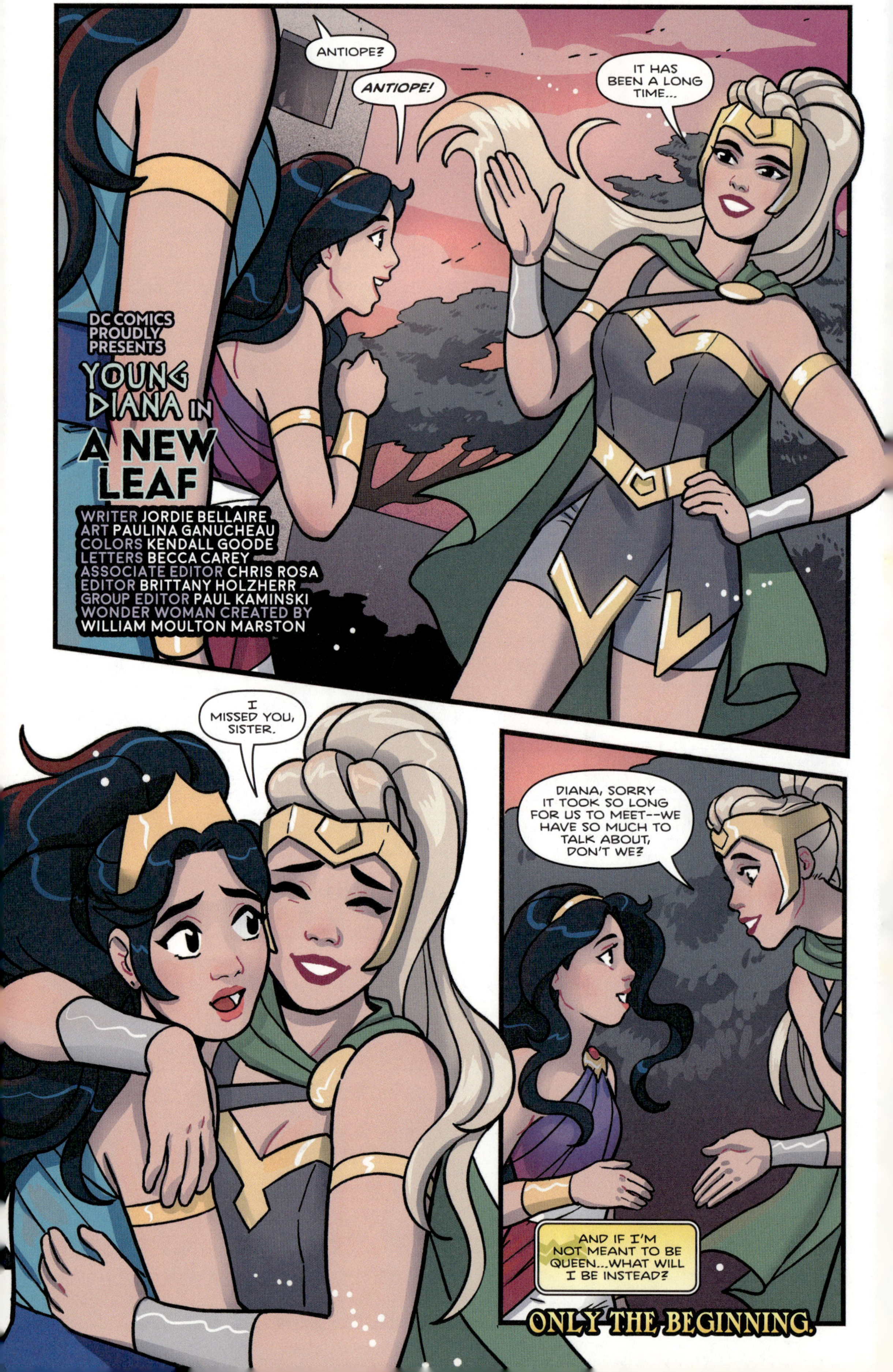
ANTIOPE?
ANTIOPE!
IT HAS BEEN A LONG TIME...
DC COMICS PROUDLY PRESENTS
YOUNG DIANA IN
A NEW LEAF
WRITER JORDIE BELLAIRE
ART PAULINA GANUCHEAU
COLORS KENDALL GOODE
LETTERS BECCA CAREY
ASSOCIATE EDITOR CHRIS ROSA
EDITOR BRITTANY HOLZHERR
GROUP EDITOR PAUL KAMINSKI
WONDER WOMAN CREATED BY WILLIAM MOULTON MARSTON
I MISSED YOU, SISTER.
DIANA, SORRY IT TOOK SO LONG FOR US TO MEET--WE HAVE SO MUCH TO TALK ABOUT, DON'T WE?
AND IF I'M NOT MEANT TO BE QUEEN...WHAT WILL I BE INSTEAD?
ONLY THE BEGINNING.

*Trial of the Amazons* #1 cover by Jim Cheung and Jay David Ramos

*Trial of the Amazons #1 variant cover by Rose Besch*

THEMYSCIRA.
I BELIEVE PENELOPE'S VISION OF OUR ISLAND BURNING IS MORE OF A FOREWARNING THAN ANYTHING ELSE--ESPECIALLY WITH PRINCESS DIANA NOW BACK.
I TRUST THE SAME IS TRUE, BIA. BUT THE ANIMALS...COULD THEY REPRESENT US? YOU SAID THERE WAS A JAGUAR PRESENT, PENELOPE?
YES, QUEEN.
HMM...A CONNECTION TO *YARA FLOR?*
IT IS POSSIBLE, JUST AS THE LIONS MIGHT CONNECT TO THEMYSCIRA.
*HIPPOLYTA* MUST KNOW MORE THAN SHE IS LETTING ON.
AND IF THE AMAZON WERE TO MAKE HERSELF KNOWN AT THE EMBASSY?
SHE WILL BE WELCOMED AS OUR SISTER UNLESS SHE GIVES US REASON TO FEEL OTHERWISE.
FOR NOW, WE WILL FOCUS ON THE CONTEST CEREMONIES AND PRINCESS DIANA'S RETURN TO THE MORTAL PLANE.
HIPPOLYTA, IF I COULD HAVE A FEW MORE MINUTES OF YOUR TIME?
MOST CERTAINLY, YOUR HIGHNESS.

ELSEWHERE.
WHAT ABOUT THE KANGA IN THE LAST STABLE? IS IT OKAY?
OH JUMPA? THAT IS ONE OF DIANA'S OLDEST FRIENDS. SHE HASN'T WANTED TO DO MUCH SINCE THE PRINCESS LEFT.
SHARP ENOUGH TO SPLIT A FROG HAIR. PERFECT.
WHAT'S TROUBLING YOU, MEDUSA?
I'VE BEEN CALLED TO MEET WITH QUEEN NUBIA LATER TODAY. WHAT IF SHE'S CHANGED HER MIND NOW THAT HIPPOLYTA IS BACK?
WHAT IF SHE SENDS ME BACK BEHIND THE DOOR-WAY?
SHE WOULDN'T.
IF I CAN OFFER SOME SISTERLY ADVICE?

ARE EITHER OF YOU THINKING OF PARTICIPATING?
SEEMS LIKE IT COULD BE A BIT OF FUN.
I'M NOT SURE ABOUT THE FUN PART, BUT IT SOUNDS *DANGEROUS* SO I'M IN.
HOW IS THE FEAST PREPARATION GOING?
GREAT! I HAVE A FEW MORE BASKETS TO TAKE BACK TO THE PALACE.
PLEASE.
FOCUS ON WHAT YOU NOW HAVE THE FREEDOM TO DO.

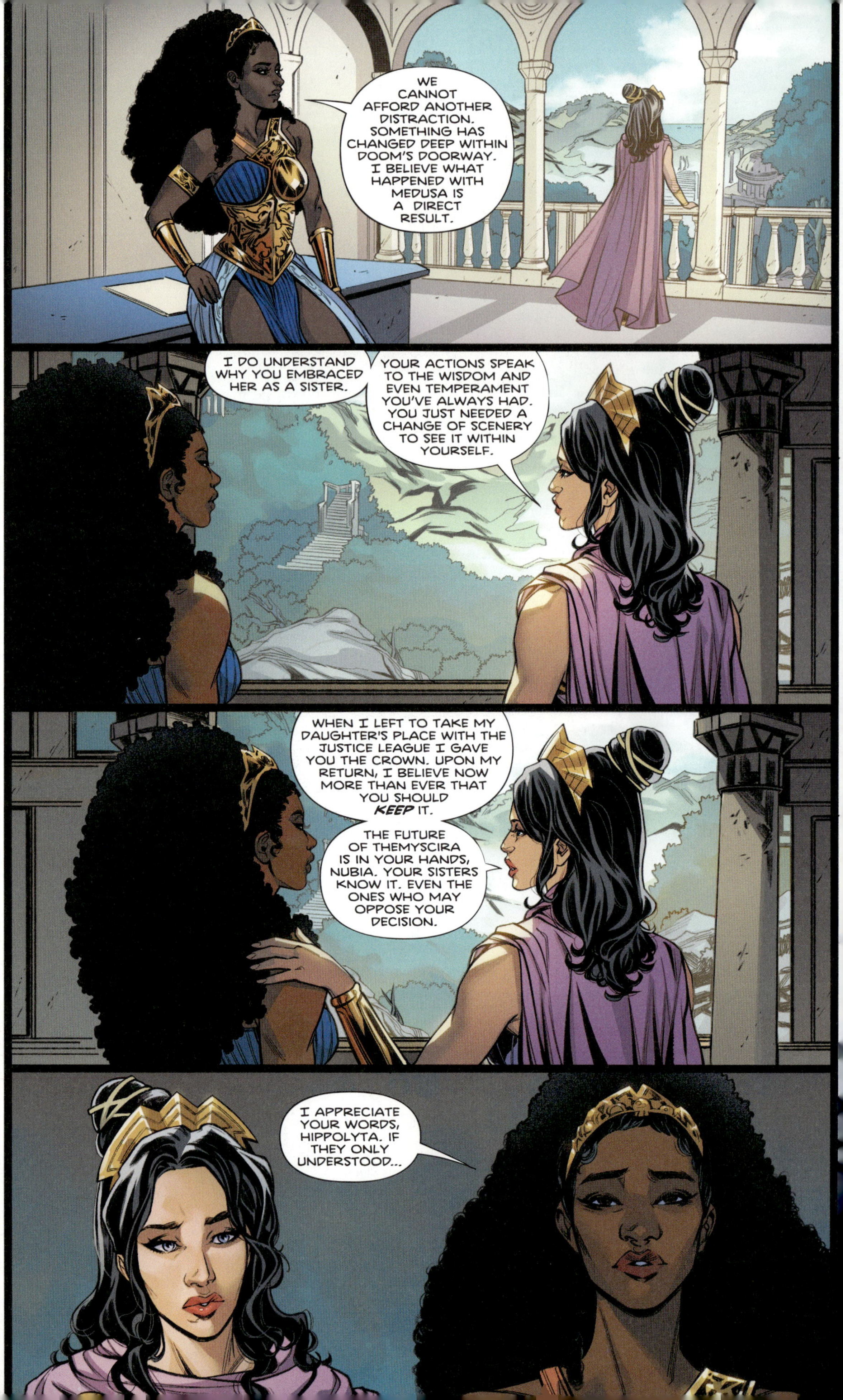

WE CANNOT AFFORD ANOTHER DISTRACTION. SOMETHING HAS CHANGED DEEP WITHIN DOOM'S DOORWAY. I BELIEVE WHAT HAPPENED WITH MEDUSA IS A DIRECT RESULT.
I DO UNDERSTAND WHY YOU EMBRACED HER AS A SISTER.
YOUR ACTIONS SPEAK TO THE WISDOM AND EVEN TEMPERAMENT YOU'VE ALWAYS HAD. YOU JUST NEEDED A CHANGE OF SCENERY TO SEE IT WITHIN YOURSELF.
WHEN I LEFT TO TAKE MY DAUGHTER'S PLACE WITH THE JUSTICE LEAGUE I GAVE YOU THE CROWN. UPON MY RETURN, I BELIEVE NOW MORE THAN EVER THAT YOU SHOULD *KEEP* IT.
THE FUTURE OF THEMYSCIRA IS IN YOUR HANDS, NUBIA. YOUR SISTERS KNOW IT. EVEN THE ONES WHO MAY OPPOSE YOUR DECISION.
I APPRECIATE YOUR WORDS, HIPPOLYTA. IF THEY ONLY UNDERSTOOD...

"...MEDUSA IS THE LEAST OF OUR WORRIES."
THE AMAZON EMBASSY. BOSTON HARBOR.
YOU CAN'T JUST BARGE IN HERE UNINVITED!
WE'RE *AMAZONS*, THAT'S ALL THE INVITATION WE NEED.
THEN YOU WILL NEED TO SURRENDER YOUR WEAPONS.

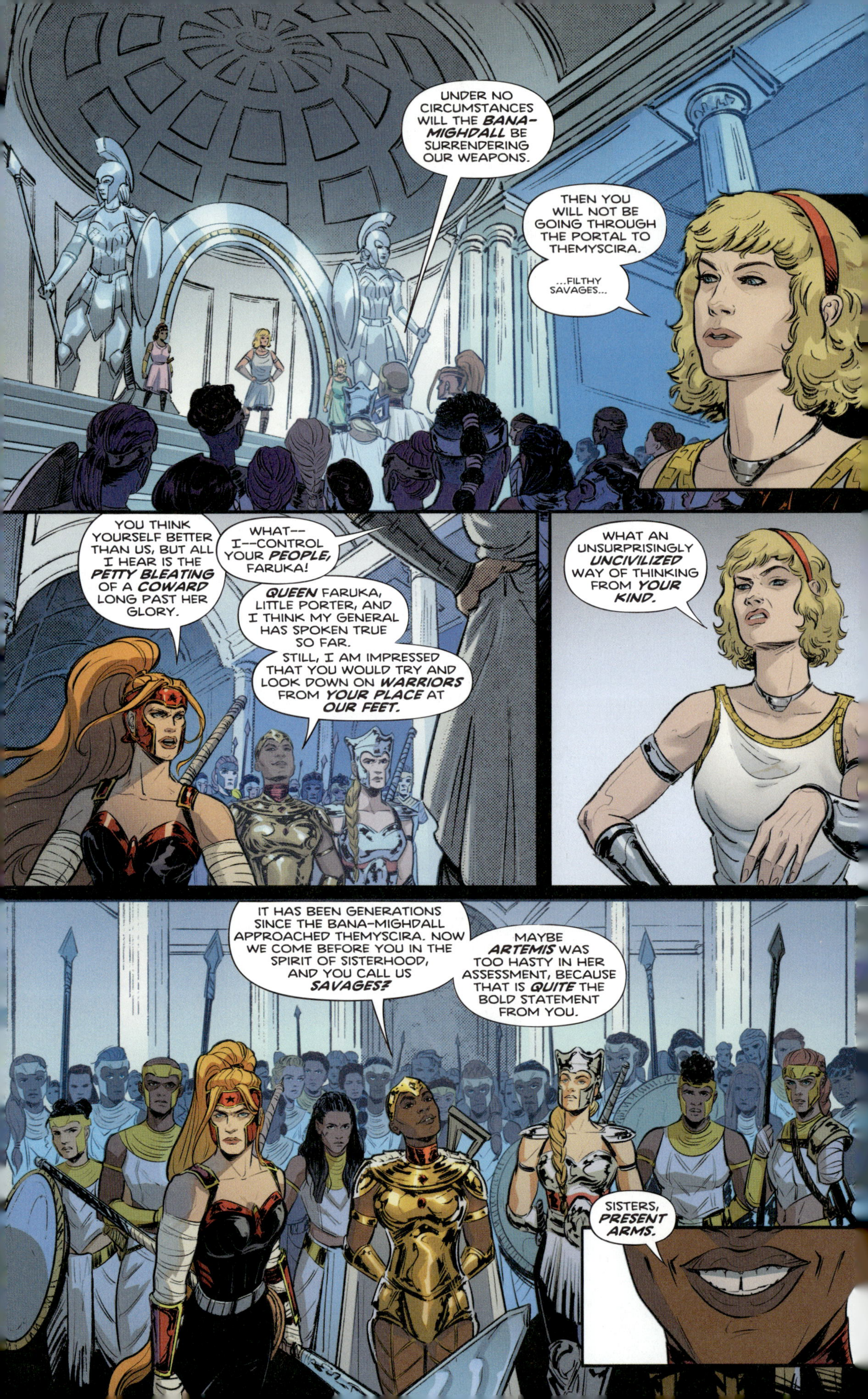
UNDER NO CIRCUMSTANCES WILL THE BANA-MIGHDALL BE SURRENDERING OUR WEAPONS.
THEN YOU WILL NOT BE GOING THROUGH THE PORTAL TO THEMYSCIRA.
...FILTHY SAVAGES...
YOU THINK YOURSELF BETTER THAN US, BUT ALL I HEAR IS THE PETTY BLEATING OF A COWARD LONG PAST HER GLORY.
WHAT-- I--CONTROL YOUR PEOPLE, FARUKA!
QUEEN FARUKA, LITTLE PORTER, AND I THINK MY GENERAL HAS SPOKEN TRUE SO FAR.
STILL, I AM IMPRESSED THAT YOU WOULD TRY AND LOOK DOWN ON WARRIORS FROM YOUR PLACE AT OUR FEET.
WHAT AN UNSURPRISINGLY UNCIVILIZED WAY OF THINKING FROM YOUR KIND.
IT HAS BEEN GENERATIONS SINCE THE BANA-MIGHDALL APPROACHED THEMYSCIRA. NOW WE COME BEFORE YOU IN THE SPIRIT OF SISTERHOOD, AND YOU CALL US SAVAGES?
MAYBE ARTEMIS WAS TOO HASTY IN HER ASSESSMENT, BECAUSE THAT IS QUITE THE BOLD STATEMENT FROM YOU.
SISTERS, PRESENT ARMS.

YOU WILL GET OUR WEAPONS WHEN YOU PRY THEM FROM OUR BLOODY, TWITCHING FINGERS.
I WELCOME YOUR EFFORT-- COME FORWARD IF YOU WISH TO FEEL HOW SAVAGE WE CAN BE.
YOU THREATEN WAR AT AN EMBASSY OF PEACE.
WE DO NOT THREATEN ANYTHING, ONLY PROMISE--
--KALLIOPE SURELY RECOGNIZES HER ERROR.
THERE IS NO AMAZON LAW THAT WOULD REQUIRE US TO DISARM OURSELVES TO ENTER OUR OWN HOMELAND.
BUT--
YOU WILL STAND ASIDE AND ALLOW US TO ENTER.
UNLESS YOU HAVE THE AUTHORITY TO EXILE FELLOW AMAZONS?
SISTER.

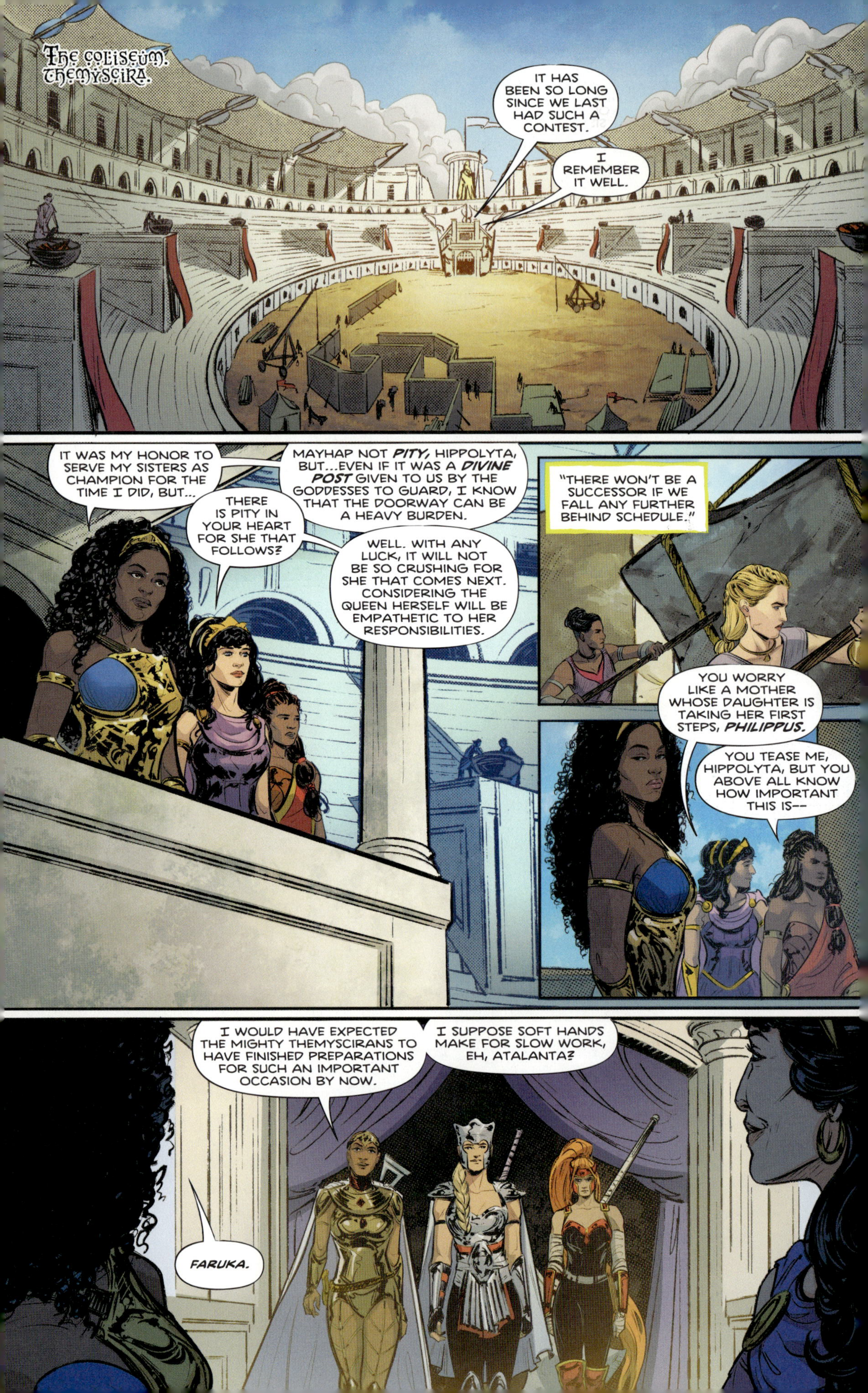
The Coliseum. Themyscira.
IT HAS BEEN SO LONG SINCE WE LAST HAD SUCH A CONTEST.
I REMEMBER IT WELL.
IT WAS MY HONOR TO SERVE MY SISTERS AS CHAMPION FOR THE TIME I DID, BUT...
THERE IS PITY IN YOUR HEART FOR SHE THAT FOLLOWS?
MAYHAP NOT PITY, HIPPOLYTA, BUT...EVEN IF IT WAS A DIVINE POST GIVEN TO US BY THE GODDESSES TO GUARD, I KNOW THAT THE DOORWAY CAN BE A HEAVY BURDEN.
WELL. WITH ANY LUCK, IT WILL NOT BE SO CRUSHING FOR SHE THAT COMES NEXT. CONSIDERING THE QUEEN HERSELF WILL BE EMPATHETIC TO HER RESPONSIBILITIES.
"THERE WON'T BE A SUCCESSOR IF WE FALL ANY FURTHER BEHIND SCHEDULE."
YOU WORRY LIKE A MOTHER WHOSE DAUGHTER IS TAKING HER FIRST STEPS, PHILIPPUS.
YOU TEASE ME, HIPPOLYTA, BUT YOU ABOVE ALL KNOW HOW IMPORTANT THIS IS--
I WOULD HAVE EXPECTED THE MIGHTY THEMYSCIRANS TO HAVE FINISHED PREPARATIONS FOR SUCH AN IMPORTANT OCCASION BY NOW.
I SUPPOSE SOFT HANDS MAKE FOR SLOW WORK, EH, ATALANTA?
FARUKA.

SISTER, IT HAS BEEN TOO LONG.
IT IS GOOD TO HAVE YOU HERE, SISTER.
WE ARE HONORED FOR YOUR PRESENCE HERE, ATALANTA.
THE HONOR IS MINE, NUBIA. BUT I SEE THE QUESTION IN YOUR EYES.
TO ANSWER IT, THE BANA-MIGHDALL ARE HERE TO TAKE PART IN THE CONTEST FOR CHAMPION.
"AND IT IS AN HONOR TO HAVE YOU AS WELL, QUEEN FARUKA OF THE BANA-MIGHDALL."
WHY THANK YOU, NUBIA, FORMER CHAMPION OF DOOM'S DOORWAY.
IT IS ALWAYS AN OCCASION TO SHARE SPACE WITH YOU, QUEEN FARUKA.
THOUGH I AM SURPRISED TO HEAR WHY YOU HAVE GRACED US WITH A VISIT.
ARE YOU NOW?
DOES IT REALLY SURPRISE YOU THAT WE COME TO CLAIM THE TITLE OF CHAMPION, WHEN THE LEAST EXPERIENCED OF THE BANA-MIGHDALL COULD BEST THEMYSCIRA'S MOST ROBUST WARRIOR, ON ANY BATTLEFIELD?
LACKING SCRUPLES AND GLORIFYING VIOLENCE AND BLOODSHED DOES NOT MAKE ONE A MORE EFFECTIVE WARRIOR.
NOR DOES IT MAKE SOMEONE WORTHY OF BEING CHAMPION OF DOOM'S DOORWAY.
THEMYSCIRAN LIFE HAS MADE YOUR PEOPLE UNFIT--OTHERWISE, HOW ELSE WOULD THE BEAST HAVE ESCAPED AND CAUSED HAVOC IN MAN'S WORLD?
NO. YOUR PEOPLE CANNOT BE TRUSTED TO DO WHAT NEEDS TO BE DONE AT THE DOOR TO TARTARUS.
OF WHAT DO YOU SPEAK, FARUKA? BE PLAIN.
THE MANTICORE. IT ATTACKED OUR COMPOUND IN QURAC.*
*SEE WONDER WOMAN #781-784! --BRITTANY
IT WAS ATALANTA WHO CONVINCED ME IT WAS NOT AN ACT OF ALL-OUT WAR ON THE PART OF THEMYSCIRA. SO, IT MUST THEN BE GROSS INEPTITUDE.
UNLESS SHE WAS WRONG?

WE...WERE UNAWARE OF THE BREACH.
IT MUST HAVE OCCURRED WHEN WE WERE DEALING WITH MEDUSA.*
MY DEEPEST APOLOGIES FOR ANY SUFFERING THAT WAS CAUSED--
*SEE NUBIA & THE AMAZONS! -- BRITTANY
HMPH.
PATHETIC.
MY QUEEN--
--BE STILL, ARTEMIS. I STAND FOR HILDA, WHO LOST AN ARM, AND RHEA WHO ALMOST LOST HER LIFE BECAUSE OF THEMYSCIRAN DISDAIN.
WHILE I WOULD SPEAK FALSE IF I SAID THERE WAS NOTHING BUT LOVE BETWEEN OUR PEOPLE--
--YOU HAVE MY WORD AS QUEEN AND FORMER CHAMPION THAT I WOULD NEVER WILLINGLY ALLOW HARM TO COME TO YOU AND YOURS.
INEPTITUDE IT IS, THEN.
WATCH YOUR TONGUE, OUTSIDER--
--THE SOLUTION IS CLEAR. PLACE A BANA-MIGHDALL AT THE DOOR WHILE WE PLAY IN YOUR LITTLE COLISEUM.
AND WHEN THIS FARCE OF A CONTEST IS OVER, ALL WILL SEE WHO THE TRUE AMAZONS ARE.
AHEM.
YEAH, ABOUT THAT...

...WE TOO ARE...
...AMAZONS?
WHAT?

ALALALA!
WHAT IS THE MEANING OF THIS?

MY NAME IS YARA FLOR, OF THE ESQUECIDA TRIBE. I DEMAND TO SPEAK TO WHOEVER RUNS THIS JOINT!
YOU MAKE DEMANDS OF ME?!
IT WOULD BE BEST THAT YOU TAKE YOUR MUTATION OF A PET HORSE AND FLY BACK TO WHEREVER YOU CAME FROM BEFORE YOU GET HURT!
WHINNY
DON'T DO IT, JERRY! SHE'S NOT WORTH IT, LET ME HANDLE THIS!
YOU BEST MOVE OUT OF MY WAY BEFORE I MAKE YOU!
MAKE ME?! YOU AND WHAT ARMY... GIRL?!
WHISTLE!

SO GLAD YOU ASKED! LET ME INTRODUCE YOU TO THE ESQUECIDA!

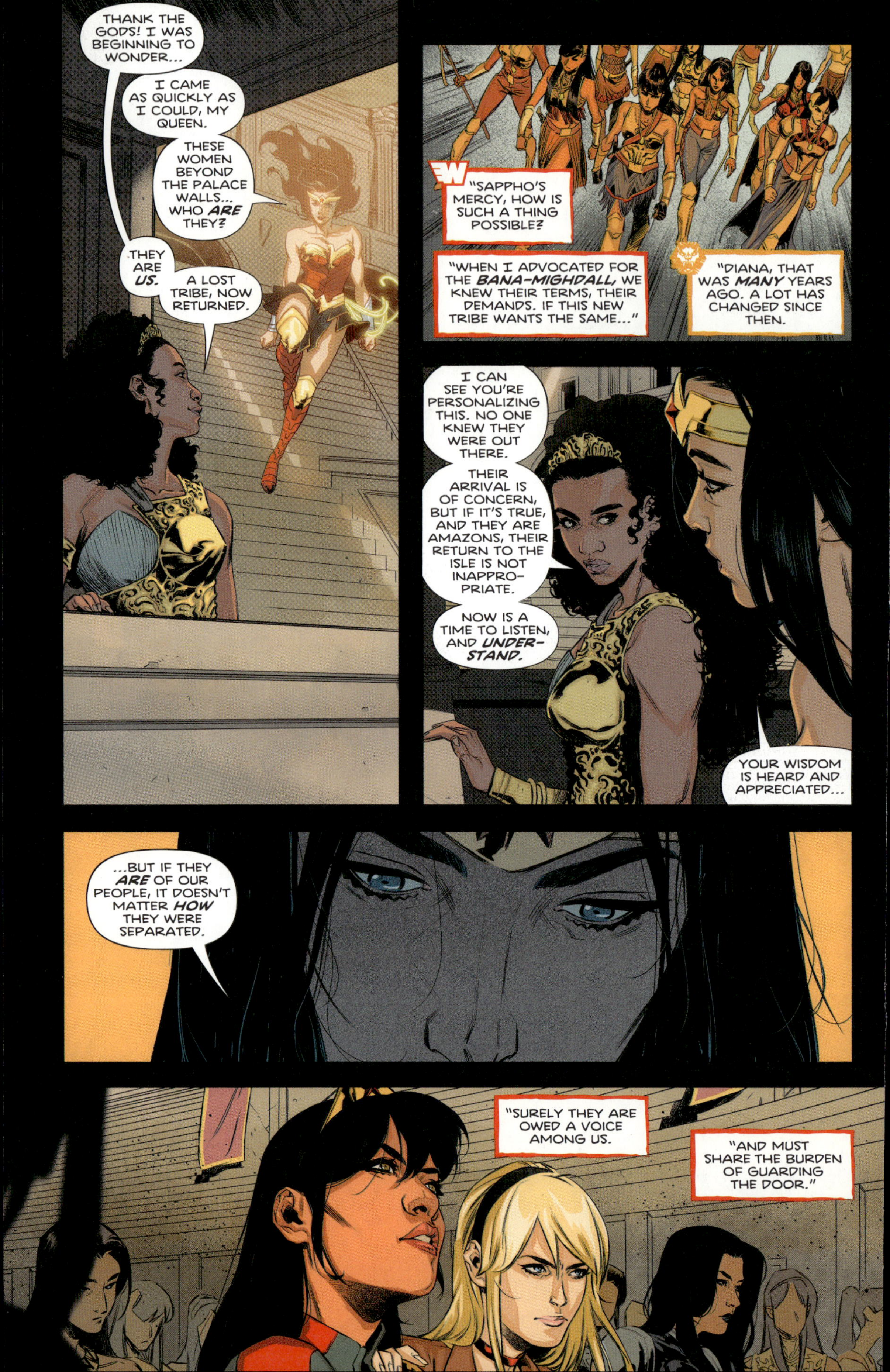

THANK THE GODS! I WAS BEGINNING TO WONDER...
I CAME AS QUICKLY AS I COULD, MY QUEEN.
THESE WOMEN BEYOND THE PALACE WALLS... WHO ARE THEY?
THEY ARE US.
A LOST TRIBE, NOW RETURNED.
"SAPPHO'S MERCY, HOW IS SUCH A THING POSSIBLE?
"WHEN I ADVOCATED FOR THE BANA-MIGHDALL, WE KNEW THEIR TERMS, THEIR DEMANDS. IF THIS NEW TRIBE WANTS THE SAME..."
"DIANA, THAT WAS MANY YEARS AGO. A LOT HAS CHANGED SINCE THEN.
I CAN SEE YOU'RE PERSONALIZING THIS. NO ONE KNEW THEY WERE OUT THERE.
THEIR ARRIVAL IS OF CONCERN, BUT IF IT'S TRUE, AND THEY ARE AMAZONS, THEIR RETURN TO THE ISLE IS NOT INAPPROPRIATE.
NOW IS A TIME TO LISTEN, AND UNDERSTAND.
YOUR WISDOM IS HEARD AND APPRECIATED...
...BUT IF THEY ARE OF OUR PEOPLE, IT DOESN'T MATTER HOW THEY WERE SEPARATED.
"SURELY THEY ARE OWED A VOICE AMONG US.
"AND MUST SHARE THE BURDEN OF GUARDING THE DOOR."

I WILL GO MEET THEM--
NO, DIANA. THEY WILL MEET YOU.
WE SHALL HOLD A DIPLOMATIC ASSEMBLY TO HEAR THEIR CLAIMS, AFTER WE HONOR THEIR ARRIVAL WITH A FEAST.
THE BANA-MIGHDALL WILL TAKE UMBRAGE OF COURSE, AS ONE MIGHT EXPECT FROM A TRIBE THAT HAS BEEN SO ROUNDLY DISMISSED IN THE PAST...
AS YOU CAN SEE, A LOT RIDES ON THIS NEW CONTEST.
THE TRIAL WILL DETERMINE THE FUTURE, NOT JUST OF THEMYSCIRA, BUT OF ALL AMAZONS.
OF COURSE, YOU'RE RIGHT. I SHOULD PROBABLY FIND MY MOTHER ANYWAY.
I TRUST SHE'S BEEN WELL SINCE RETURNING FROM MAN'S WORLD?
HAH! MAN'S WORLD. FROM WHAT HIPPOLYTA HAS TOLD ME, THINGS ARE CHANGING--SOON WE'LL BE CALLING IT CORPORATION WORLD, OR SOME SUCH!
SHE IS WELL, AND YES, GLAD TO BE HOME.
I KNOW I'M NOT ALWAYS THE MOST PRESENT MEMBER OF OUR FAMILY, BUT I AM HERE NOW, MY QUEEN. IF THERE IS ANYTHING I CAN DO...
GOOD. THEN I SHALL GO TO HER.
HUSH, SISTER. YOU THINK I REQUIRE YOUR SERVICE? I'M WELL SERVED.
HA HA!

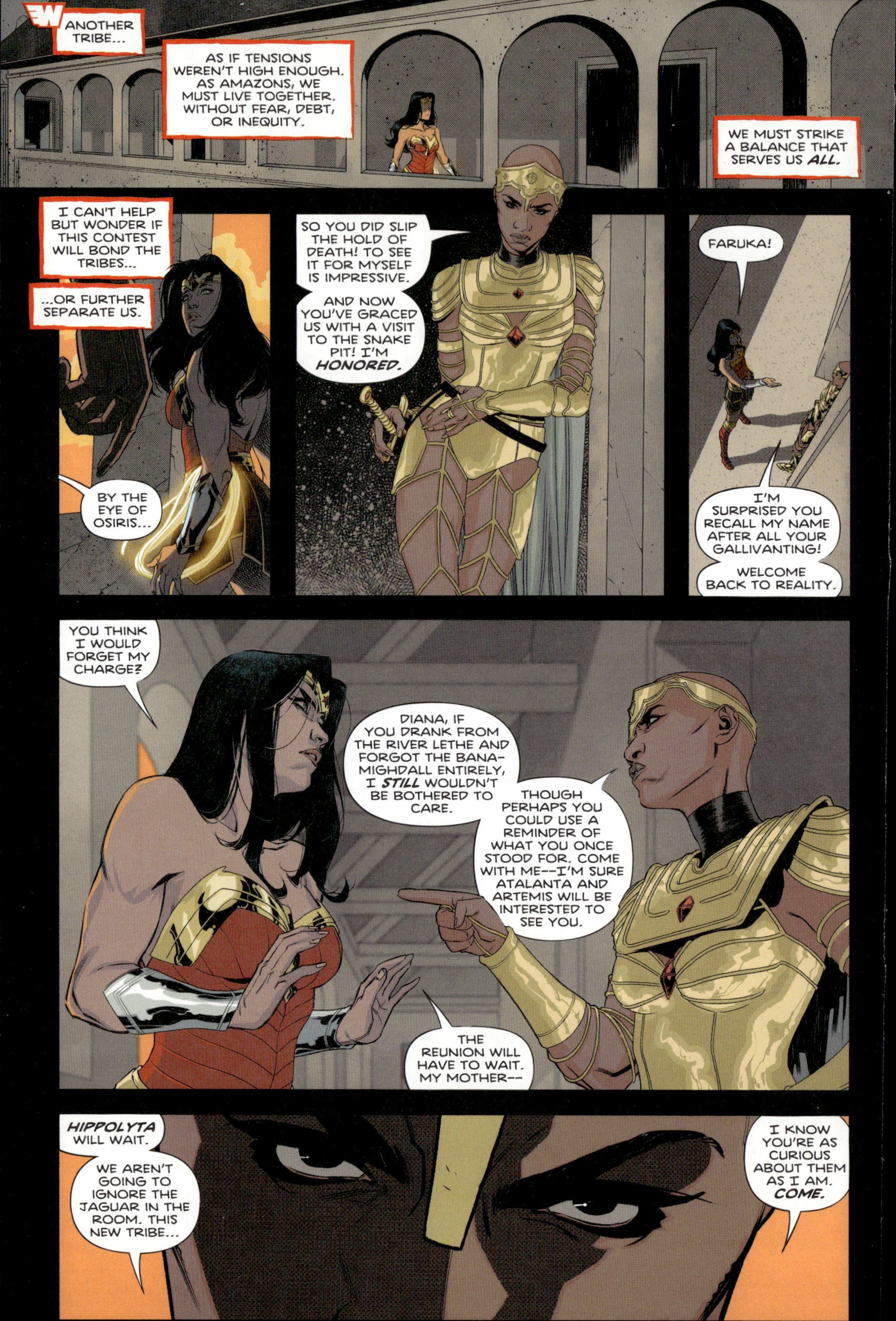
ANOTHER TRIBE...
AS IF TENSIONS WEREN'T HIGH ENOUGH. AS AMAZONS, WE MUST LIVE TOGETHER. WITHOUT FEAR, DEBT, OR INEQUITY.
WE MUST STRIKE A BALANCE THAT SERVES US ALL.
I CAN'T HELP BUT WONDER IF THIS CONTEST WILL BOND THE TRIBES...
...OR FURTHER SEPARATE US.
BY THE EYE OF OSIRIS...
SO YOU DID SLIP THE HOLD OF DEATH! TO SEE IT FOR MYSELF IS IMPRESSIVE.
AND NOW YOU'VE GRACED US WITH A VISIT TO THE SNAKE PIT! I'M HONORED.
FARUKA!
I'M SURPRISED YOU RECALL MY NAME AFTER ALL YOUR GALLIVANTING!
WELCOME BACK TO REALITY.
YOU THINK I WOULD FORGET MY CHARGE?
DIANA, IF YOU DRANK FROM THE RIVER LETHE AND FORGOT THE BANA-MIGHDALL ENTIRELY, I STILL WOULDN'T BE BOTHERED TO CARE.
THOUGH PERHAPS YOU COULD USE A REMINDER OF WHAT YOU ONCE STOOD FOR. COME WITH ME--I'M SURE ATALANTA AND ARTEMIS WILL BE INTERESTED TO SEE YOU.
THE REUNION WILL HAVE TO WAIT. MY MOTHER--
HIPPOLYTA WILL WAIT.
WE AREN'T GOING TO IGNORE THE JAGUAR IN THE ROOM. THIS NEW TRIBE...
I KNOW YOU'RE AS CURIOUS ABOUT THEM AS I AM. COME.

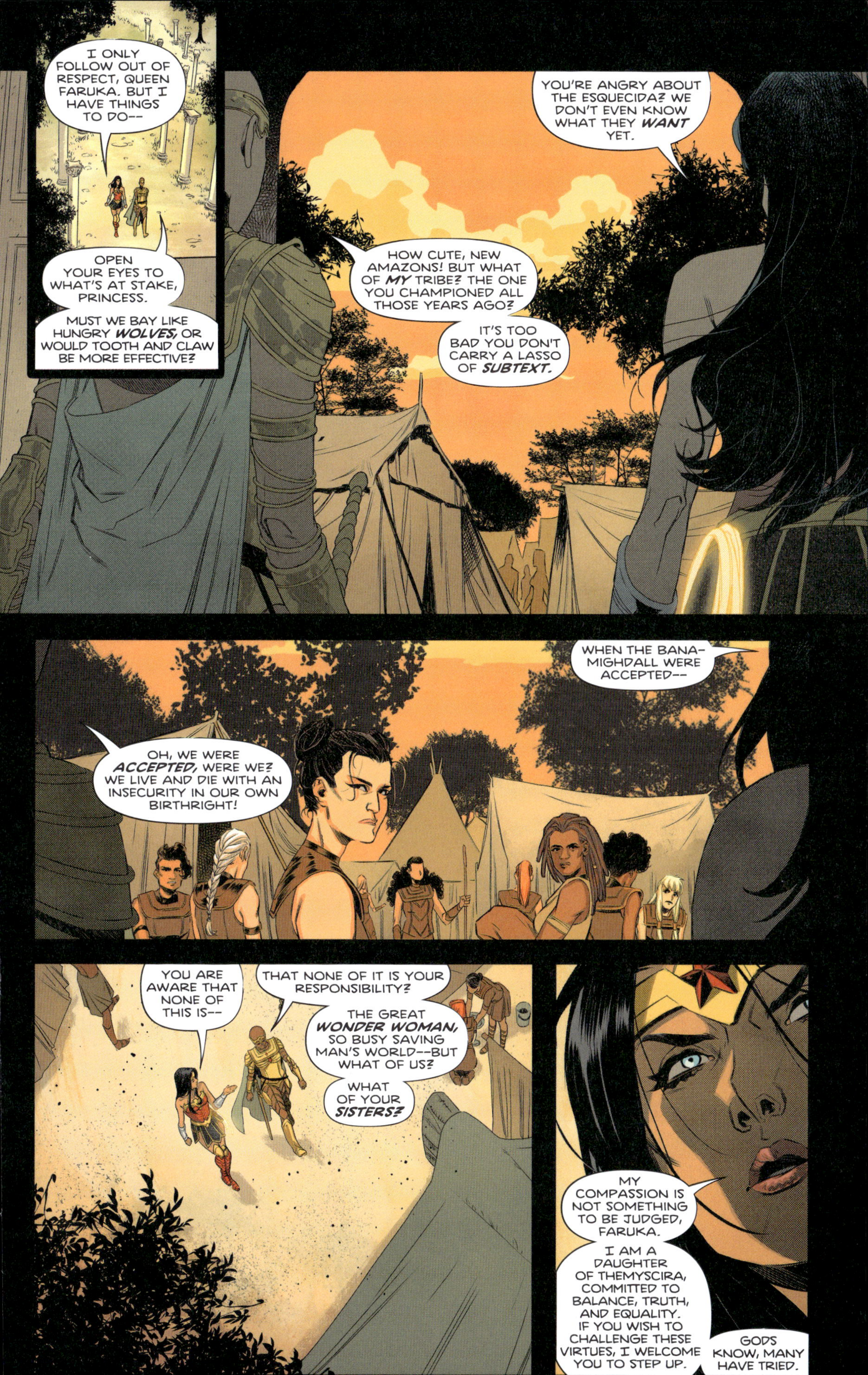
I ONLY FOLLOW OUT OF RESPECT, QUEEN FARUKA. BUT I HAVE THINGS TO DO--
OPEN YOUR EYES TO WHAT'S AT STAKE, PRINCESS.
MUST WE BAY LIKE HUNGRY WOLVES, OR WOULD TOOTH AND CLAW BE MORE EFFECTIVE?
YOU'RE ANGRY ABOUT THE ESQUECIDA? WE DON'T EVEN KNOW WHAT THEY WANT YET.
HOW CUTE, NEW AMAZONS! BUT WHAT OF MY TRIBE? THE ONE YOU CHAMPIONED ALL THOSE YEARS AGO?
IT'S TOO BAD YOU DON'T CARRY A LASSO OF SUBTEXT.
WHEN THE BANA-MIGHDALL WERE ACCEPTED--
OH, WE WERE ACCEPTED, WERE WE? WE LIVE AND DIE WITH AN INSECURITY IN OUR OWN BIRTHRIGHT!
YOU ARE AWARE THAT NONE OF THIS IS--
THAT NONE OF IT IS YOUR RESPONSIBILITY?
THE GREAT WONDER WOMAN, SO BUSY SAVING MAN'S WORLD--BUT WHAT OF US?
WHAT OF YOUR SISTERS?
MY COMPASSION IS NOT SOMETHING TO BE JUDGED, FARUKA.
I AM A DAUGHTER OF THEMYSCIRA, COMMITTED TO BALANCE, TRUTH, AND EQUALITY. IF YOU WISH TO CHALLENGE THESE VIRTUES, I WELCOME YOU TO STEP UP.
GODS KNOW, MANY HAVE TRIED.

I DON'T NEED DIVINE SIGHT TO KNOW I'D SIT YOU DOWN.
TAKE UP ARMS, THEN! LET'S SEE HOW IT PLAYS!
I WON'T REQUIRE WEAPONS FOR THIS SPARRING MATCH.
VERY WELL, THEN...
...ALLOW ME TO SHOW YOU WHY YOU'LL NEVER BE A *QUEEN!*
YOU SUGGEST I *DESIRE* SUCH A BURDEN!
WHAT I *SUGGEST* IS--
QUEEN FARUKA! PRINCESS DIANA!
APOLOGIES FOR INTERRUPTING.
THE FEAST WILL BEGIN MOMENTARILY... I WAS SENT TO FETCH YOU.
HAH. IT IS GOOD TO HAVE YOU BACK, MY SISTER. THE WORLD WASN'T THE SAME WITHOUT YOU.
THAT SAID, YOU OWE ME A PROPER FIGHT.
I LOOK FORWARD TO IT. NOW LET US JOIN THE OTHERS.

DOOM'S DOORWAY.
NOT MUCH FARTHER...
SHAAA SHAA SHAAA
?
IO, MEET RHEA AND YARIMA.
AS REPRESENTATIVES OF THE BANA-MIGHDALL AND ESQUECIDA RESPECTIVELY, THEY WILL BE YOUR COUNTERPARTS FOR YOUR TIME AT THE DOORWAY.
AT LEAST UNTIL THIS IS ALL SETTLED.
MY QUEEN.
I STOOD AS CHAMPION OF THIS PLACE FOR...A LONG TIME.
I, MORE THAN ANY OTHER, UNDERSTAND THE VALUE OF THE PRESENCE OF SISTERS ON THE WATCH. TREAT EACH OTHER AS YOU WOULD YOUR OWN.
I HAVE NOT HAD MUCH TIME TO BRIEF THEM ON THE SPECIFICS OF THE DOORWAY.
WOULD YOU MIND ENLIGHTENING THEM ON ANYTHING THEY NEED TO KNOW, IO?
...OF COURSE, MY QUEEN.
NOW MORE THAN EVER, WE MUST BE UNITED.

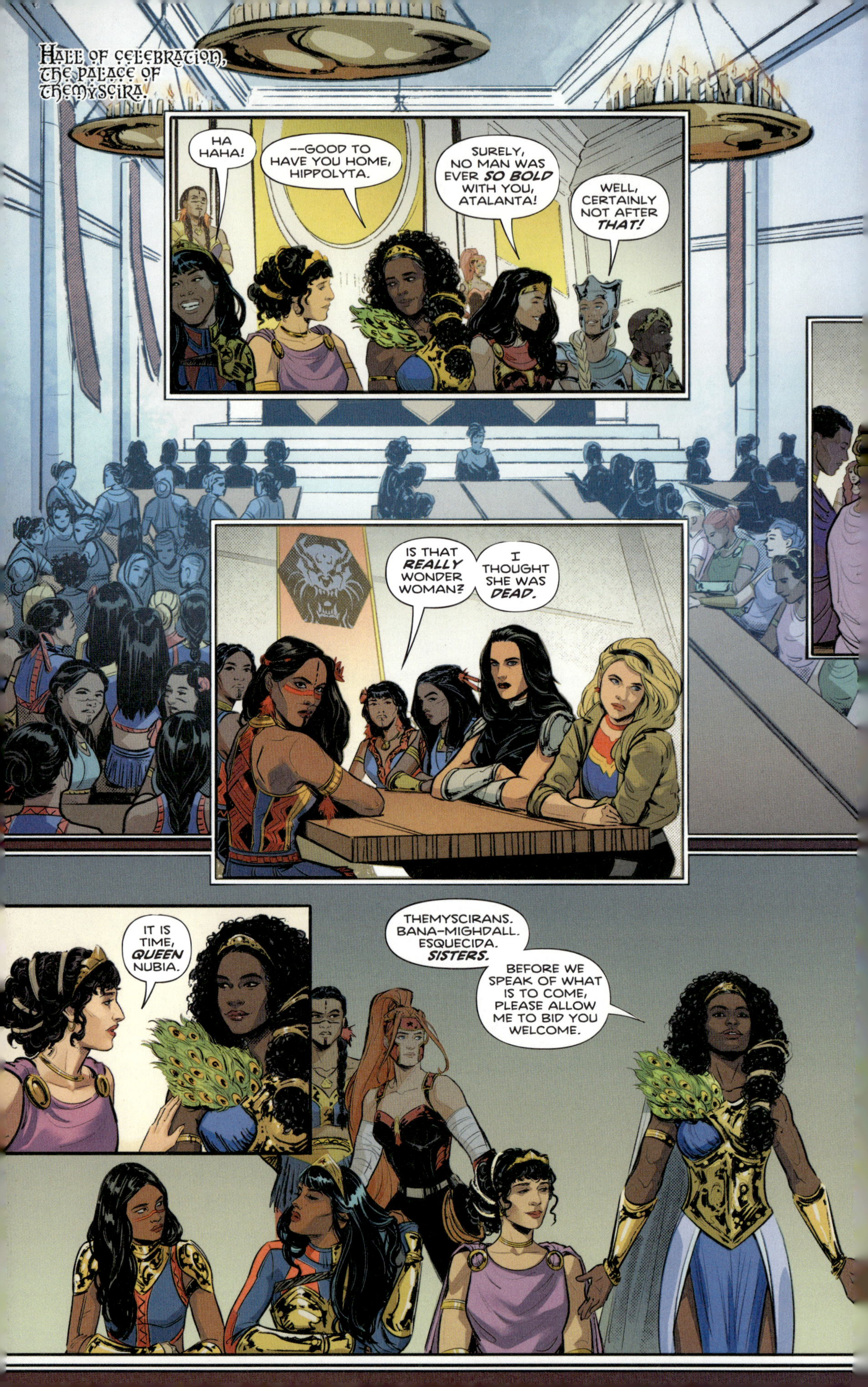
HALL OF CELEBRATION, THE PALACE OF THEMYSCIRA.
HA HAHA!
--GOOD TO HAVE YOU HOME, HIPPOLYTA.
SURELY, NO MAN WAS EVER SO BOLD WITH YOU, ATALANTA!
WELL, CERTAINLY NOT AFTER THAT!
IS THAT REALLY WONDER WOMAN?
I THOUGHT SHE WAS DEAD.
IT IS TIME, QUEEN NUBIA.
THEMYSCIRANS. BANA-MIGHDALL. ESQUECIDA. SISTERS.
BEFORE WE SPEAK OF WHAT IS TO COME, PLEASE ALLOW ME TO BID YOU WELCOME.

I HAVE A BAD FEELING. SOMETHING IS WRONG.
YES, CLEARLY SO BIA.
THE THEMYSCIRAN REALLY THOUGHT SHE COULD OUT-SHOOT YOU, BIBI?
I ALMOST FELT GUILTY COLLECTING ON THE BET!
FROM APPOINTING EMISSARIES INTO MAN'S WORLD, TO FINDING THE CHAMPION OF DOOM'S DOORWAY--ANY OTHER MATTERS IN BETWEEN--WE HAVE HELD THE CONTEST AS A SACRED RITE, MOST HOLY TO OUR PEOPLE.
WHETHER A PRINCESS, PRIESTESS, OR CARPENTER, ALL ARE EQUAL IN IN EYES OF THE DIVINE COMPETITION.
YOU ARE HERE BECAUSE, AS AMAZONS, YOU HAVE A RIGHT TO BE.
YOU ARE HERE TO PROVE YOURSELVES WORTHY TO BE CHAMPIONS.

"THE RULES ARE NOT MANY, BUT THEY ARE SACRED.
"FIRST, ANY AMAZON IS WELCOME TO ENTER, BUT SHE MUST BE SPONSORED BY AT LEAST A SCORE OF OTHERS.
"BEING CHAMPION OF DOOM'S DOORWAY IS A HEAVY BURDEN, ONE THAT CANNOT BE BORNE WITHOUT THE SUPPORT OF ONE'S SISTERS.
SECOND, THERE ARE TO BE THREE TRIALS. THESE ARE SET FORTH BY THE ORACLE, DIVINE MESSAGES FROM THE GODDESSES.
I HAVE CONSULTED WITH OUR HIGH PRIESTESS, AND SHE HAS AGREED WITH MY ASSESSMENT THAT AN ORACLE FROM *EACH TRIBE* MUST LEND HER WISDOM TO THIS TEST.
AND THIRD, ONCE BEGUN, THE CONTEST CANNOT BE ENDED EXCEPT THROUGH A COMPETITOR'S TRIUMPH.
THIS IS NOT MERELY A CUSTOM, IT IS THE WILL OF THE GODS.
CLEARLY, WITH THE ADDITION OF THE ESQUECIDA AND BANA-MIGHDALL, WE WILL HAVE TO TAKE FURTHER CONSIDERATIONS INTO ACCOUNT.
BUT, I HAVE NO DOUBT THAT WHEN THIS IS OVER, THE CHAMPION AT THE DOOR WILL BE RIGHTEOUS.
AND OUR SISTERS WILL BE SAFE.
*AHEM* SUCH WARM, *WELCOMING* WORDS.
ESPECIALLY MOVING COMING FROM A *FORMER* CHAMPION.

ONE WONDERS WHAT GREAT SERVICES SUCH A MIGHTY WARRIOR HAS PERFORMED TO BE REWARDED WITH SUCH A SHINING CROWN.
YOU DARE--
FARUKA!
AT EASE, ATALANTA. I SIMPLY POINT OUT THAT QUEEN NUBIA WELCOMES US FROM A FRESHLY ERECTED PEDESTAL.
HA HA HA HA!
QUEEN FARUKA, SPEAKER OF TRUTH!
YOU SAY THAT WE ARE ALL SISTERS HERE, THREE TRIBES BUT ONE PEOPLE?
IN OUR TRIBE, NAMES, LET ALONE TITLES, ARE NOT HANDED OUT LIKE CANDY. WE DO NOT ACKNOWLEDGE THOSE WHO HAVE NOT EARNED THEIR PLACE.
SO TELL ME. WHY SHOULD WE FOLLOW YOU?
THIS IS THE MOST SUBTLETY YOU HAVE SHOWN YET, QUEEN FARUKA OF THE BANA-MIGHDALL. WHICH IS TO SAY, THAT OF USING AN AX TO STRIKE DOWN A MOSQUITO.
BUT, TO BE SURE I HAVE UNDERSTOOD YOU.
YOU WANT THE COMPETITORS TO NOT ONLY FIGHT FOR THE ROLE OF CHAMPION, BUT FOR THEIR QUEEN'S RIGHT TO RULE ALL AMAZONS. IS THIS SO?
YOU SEEM TO HAVE UNDERSTOOD ME JUST FINE, DESPITE MY SUBTLETY.
DONE.
HMM.
LONG LIVE THE QUEEN.

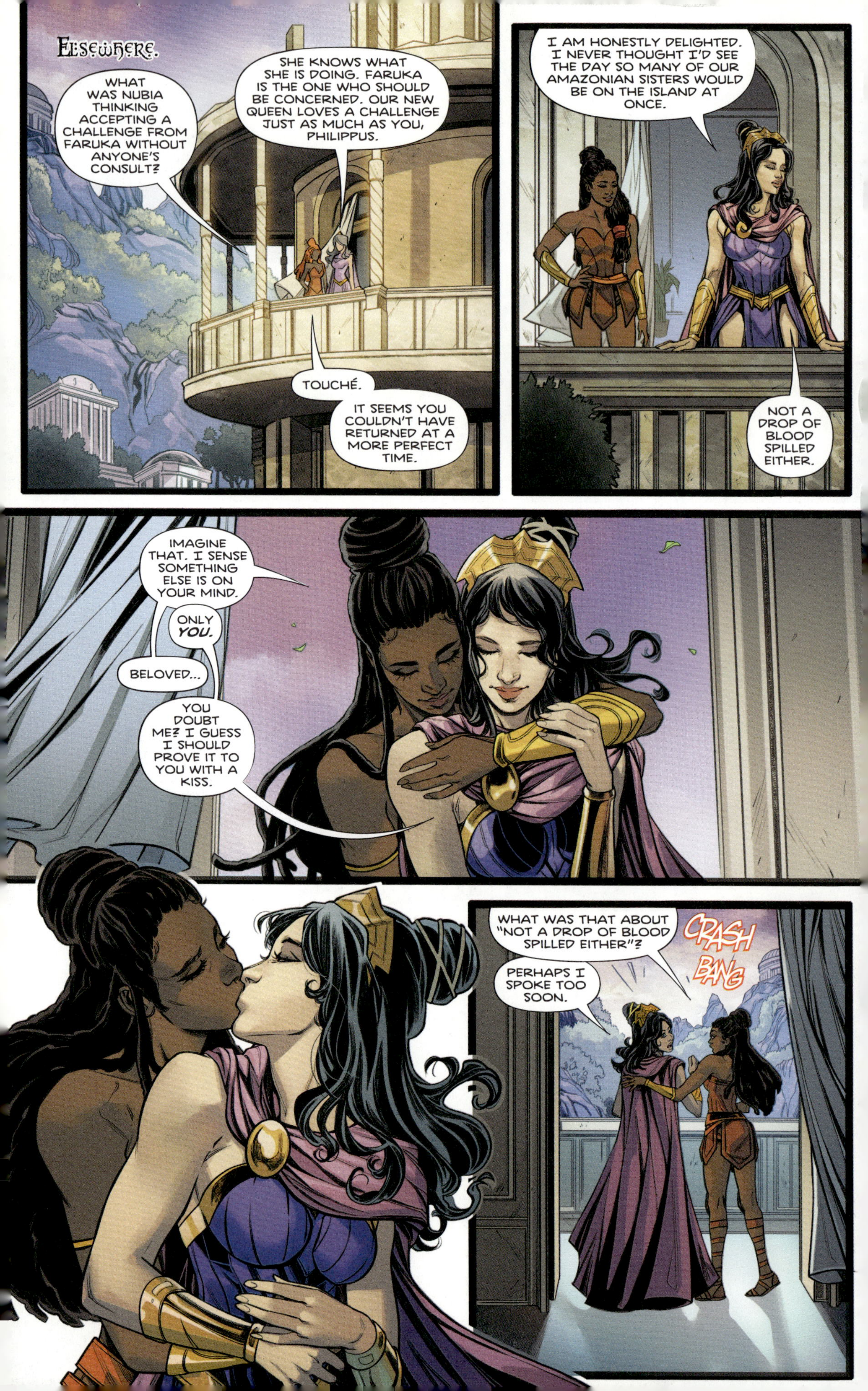
ELSEWHERE.
WHAT WAS NUBIA THINKING ACCEPTING A CHALLENGE FROM FARUKA WITHOUT ANYONE'S CONSULT?
SHE KNOWS WHAT SHE IS DOING. FARUKA IS THE ONE WHO SHOULD BE CONCERNED. OUR NEW QUEEN LOVES A CHALLENGE JUST AS MUCH AS YOU, PHILIPPUS.
TOUCHÉ.
IT SEEMS YOU COULDN'T HAVE RETURNED AT A MORE PERFECT TIME.
I AM HONESTLY DELIGHTED. I NEVER THOUGHT I'D SEE THE DAY SO MANY OF OUR AMAZONIAN SISTERS WOULD BE ON THE ISLAND AT ONCE.
NOT A DROP OF BLOOD SPILLED EITHER.
IMAGINE THAT. I SENSE SOMETHING ELSE IS ON YOUR MIND.
ONLY *YOU.*
BELOVED...
YOU DOUBT ME? I GUESS I SHOULD PROVE IT TO YOU WITH A KISS.
WHAT WAS THAT ABOUT "NOT A DROP OF BLOOD SPILLED EITHER"?
PERHAPS I SPOKE TOO SOON.
CRASH
BANG

I SHOULD GO.
OF COURSE, MY LOVE.
HOPEFULLY THE NIGHT BRINGS SOME QUIET BEFORE THE TRIALS OF TOMORROW. YOU KNOW, THERE IS A FULL MOON.
I DO.
I'LL LOOK FOR THE LIT CANDLE.
WE HAVE A BIT MORE CATCHING UP TO DO.
ENJOY THE FEAST BEFORE YOU AND COMMUNE WITH YOUR SISTERS. IT IS NOT EVERY DAY ALL THREE TRIBES ARE UNDER THE SAME ROOF. WE WILL DECIDE TOMORROW WHO WILL REPRESENT EACH TRIBE.
I AM NOT IN THE HABIT OF REPEATING MYSELF. IT WOULD BE WISE FOR ALL OF YOU TO SAVE YOUR ENERGY FOR THE COMPETITION.
PHILIPPUS, WHY ARE YOU NOT WITH HIPPOLYTA?
I WAS AFRAID THE TRIALS HAD STARTED EARLY, BUT I SEE YOU HAVE IT ALL UNDER CONTROL.
I ALWAYS DO. AS YOUR QUEEN I AM ORDERING YOU TO GO SPEND TIME WITH YOUR HEART.

LATER.
I COULD TASTE THE OMISSION OF TRUTH UPON YOUR LIPS. YOU COULD HAVE JUST TOLD ME, MY MOST CHERISHED.
I WOULD NOT HAVE WANTED TO HEAR IT, NOR WOULD I HAVE WANTED TO UNDERSTAND.
BUT I WOULD HAVE STILL TOLD YOU THAT I WILL CONTINUE LOVING YOU IN THIS REALM AND THE NEXT.
HIPPOLYTA...

IT IS ALMOST UNBELIEVABLE TO THINK TODAY HAS BEEN THE MOST EVENTFUL COMPARED TO EVERYTHING ELSE TO HAPPEN RECENTLY.
FARUKA'S BITE IS WORSE THAN A CHIMERA, BUT I CAN TELL A LOT OF IT IS REQUIRED IN MAN'S WORLD.
THOSE GODDESS-FORSAKEN BANA-MIGHDALL. THE DAY THEY LEAVE CAN'T COME SOON ENOUGH.
OH, HIPPOLYTA. I THOUGHT YOU AND PHILIPPUS MAY HAVE BEEN...
HIPPOLYTA?
NO... NO... NO...

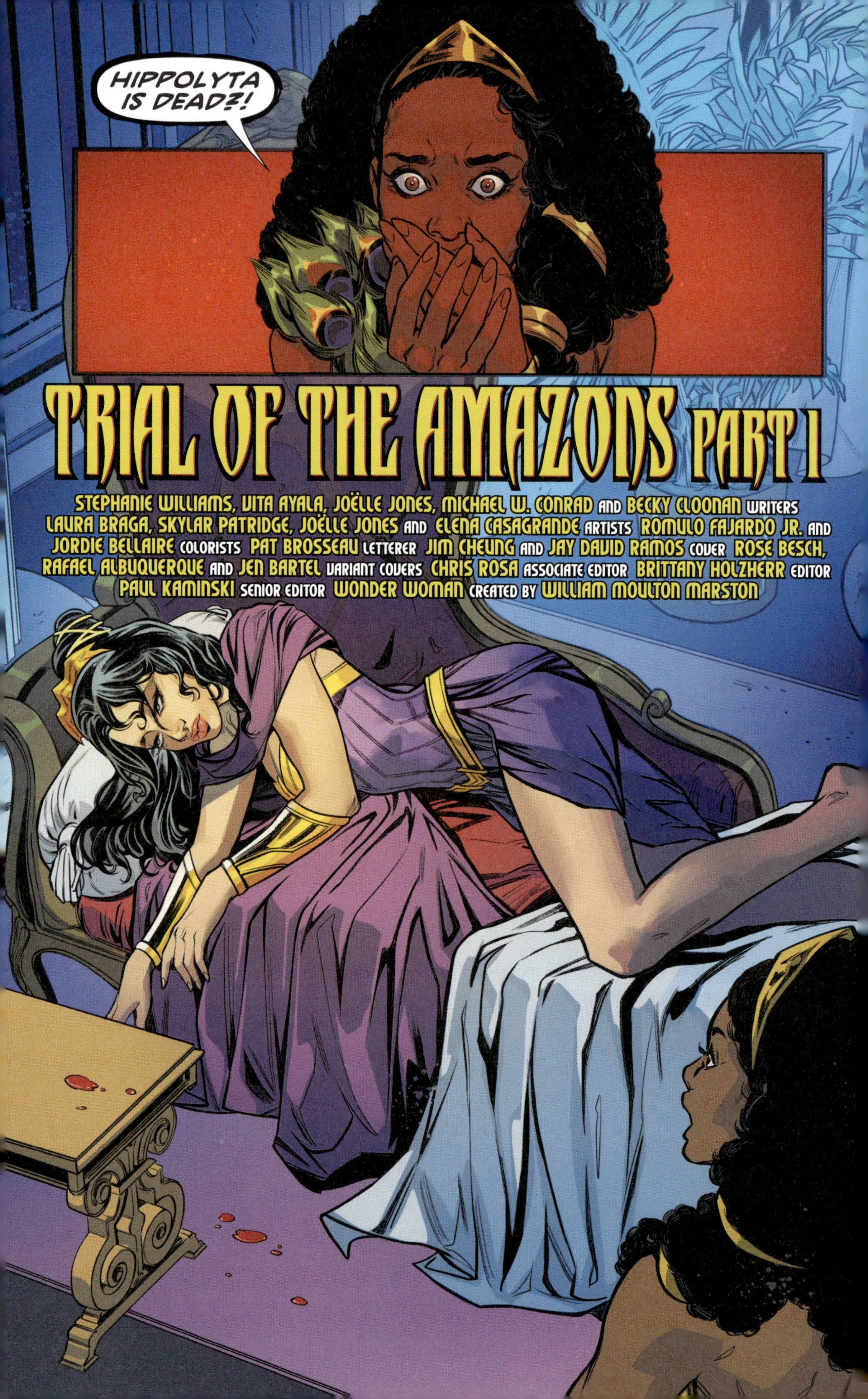

HIPPOLYTA IS DEAD?!
TRIAL OF THE AMAZONS PART 1
STEPHANIE WILLIAMS, VITA AYALA, JOËLLE JONES, MICHAEL W. CONRAD AND BECKY CLOONAN WRITERS
LAURA BRAGA, SKYLAR PATRIDGE, JOËLLE JONES AND ELENA CASAGRANDE ARTISTS ROMULO FAJARDO JR. AND
JORDIE BELLAIRE COLORISTS PAT BROSSEAU LETTERER JIM CHEUNG AND JAY DAVID RAMOS COVER ROSE BESCH,
RAFAEL ALBUQUERQUE AND JEN BARTEL VARIANT COVERS CHRIS ROSA ASSOCIATE EDITOR BRITTANY HOLZHERR EDITOR
PAUL KAMINSKI SENIOR EDITOR WONDER WOMAN CREATED BY WILLIAM MOULTON MARSTON

*Nubia & the Amazons* #6 cover by Alitha Martinez and Laura Martin

*Nubia & the Amazons* #6 variant cover by Kyle Baker

TEMPLE OF PERSEPHONE. DAYS LATER.
TRIAL OF THE AMAZONS PART 2
HIPPOLYTA WAS THE FIRST TO RISE FROM THE TURBULENT WATERS AND KISS APOLLO'S SUN-DRENCHED SKIES.
USHERED INTO A NEW LIFE THROUGH THE GUIDING VOICES OF APHRODITE, DEMETER, ATHENA, ARTEMIS, AND HESTIA, SHE WAS CHOSEN TO BE QUEEN BY THE MIDWIVES OF GAEA. IT WAS A RESPONSIBILITY HELD NOT ONLY IN THE CROWN THAT SAT UPON HER HEAD BUT ONE SHE HELD IN HER HEART.
THOUGH HIPPOLYTA'S DEPARTURE LEAVES US AT A TREMENDOUS LOSS, WE STAND TOGETHER TO GUIDE ONE OF GAEA'S BELOVED DAUGHTERS SAFELY BACK TO HER.
STEPHANIE WILLIAMS AND VITA AYALA STORY STEPHANIE WILLIAMS SCRIPT
ALITHA MARTINEZ PENCILS MARK MORALES AND ALITHA MARTINEZ INKS
ROMULO FAJARDO JR. COLORS BECCA CAREY LETTERS ALITHA MARTINEZ AND LAURA MARTIN COVER
KYLE BAKER VARIANT COVER JULIET NNEKA INTERNATIONAL WOMEN'S DAY VARIANT COVER
CHRIS ROSA ASSOCIATE EDITOR BRITTANY HOLZHERR EDITOR PAUL KAMINSKI SENIOR EDITOR

ANAHI OF THE ESQUECIDAS, YOU MAY STEP FORTH.
THANK YOU, MAGALA.
WE, THE ESQUECIDA, PROVIDE HIPPOLYTA'S FARE.
MAY THESE COINS TIP THE SCALE IN FAVOR OF A SAFE JOURNEY INTO THE AFTERLIFE.
REST WELL, SISTER.

DELPHINE OF THE THEMYSCIRANS.
I, DELPHINE, OF THE THEMYSCIRANS OFFER THIS BOUQUET.

THE ROOTS, HIPPOLYTA'S BODY, THE UNFOLDING THROUGH THE STEMS AND LEAVES, HIPPOLYTA'S SOUL, AND THE CULMINATING IN THE FLOWERS, HIPPOLYTA'S SPIRIT.
MAY PERSEPHONE BE YOUR GUIDE TO YOUR ETERNAL RESTING PLACE.

QUEEN ATALANTA AND QUEEN FARUKA OF THE BANA-MIGHDALL, YOUR BLESSINGS PLEASE.
FOR SOME, THE ABILITY TO LEAD IS IN ONE'S ESSENCE. THEREFORE, WE, THE BANA-MIGHDALL, BELIEVE THERE IS A SACRED POWER IN THE BLOOD OF THOSE WHO ARE BORN LEADERS.
WE ASK THAT EACH OF YOU CHARGED WITH THE RESPONSIBILITY OF YOUR TRIBE GIVE OF YOURSELF AND AN INVOCATION TO BRING HIPPOLYTA DIVINE SANCTION AS SHE GOES INTO THE NEXT LIFE.
ETERNAL REST UNTO YOU MY DEAR SISTER.
MAY HIPPOLYTA'S MEMORY BE EVERLASTING.

QUEEN NUBIA.
GO BRAVELY INTO THE DARKNESS WITH YOUR UNDYING LIGHT.
THE RITUAL IS COMPLETE ONCE THE VIAL IS PLACED WITH THE DEPARTED BY ONE WHOSE LOVE WILL GO ON WITH THEM WELL INTO THE NEXT LIFE.
DIANA...
THE HONOR IS YOURS, PHILIPPUS.
NO, MY DAUGHTER, IT IS BOTH OF OURS. I'M SO THANKFUL FOR ALL THE MOMENTS WE HAD TOGETHER AS A FAMILY.

I HUMBLY SUBMIT ALL MY LOVE UNTO YOU, DEAR HEART.
GOODBYE UNTIL WE SAY HELLO AGAIN.

I THANK EACH OF YOU.
NOW WE CARRY HIPPOLYTA'S BODY TO HER LAST REST IN THE PALACE.
FAREWELL, SISTER.

DOOM'S DOORWAY.
THOSE CAN GO RIGHT BY THE DOOR, KARESSI.
WHERE WOULD YOU LIKE THE EXTRA SUPPLIES?
IO, WHAT'S THE DEAL WITH THE DOOR?
WE THEMYSCIRANS WERE TASKED BY THE GODS TO BE ITS KEEPERS. IT IS A HIGH HONOR TO BE ASKED TO GUARD IT.
SOUNDS LIKE FREE LABOR TO ME.
HOPEFULLY THIS IS ENOUGH FOR ANOTHER FEW DAYS.
THANK YOU, KARESSI. I WAS GOING TO TAKE CARE OF THAT.
OH, IT'S NO TROUBLE AT ALL.
GROSS.
EVERYTHING OKAY?
YEAH.
WE CAN TAKE IT FROM HERE. THANK YOU, AGAIN, FOR YOUR HELP.
ANYTIME. STAY SAFE.

The Contest
What is the Contest?
The Contest is regarded as the highest of sacred rites among Amazons. All are on equal footing as the contest is considered a divine competition. All Amazons are welcome to enter; however, participants must be chosen at large by others.
Types of Events
No one contest consists of the same trial events as they are determined on a divine level. All contests throughout Amazonian history have always consisted of three types of tests for the skill set a champion must possess.
Types of Trial Events
◆ Logical and critical reasoning
◆ Physical strength
◆ Decision-making and judgment test

THE ROYAL PALACE. THE NEXT DAY.
THE CONTEST SHOULD BE CANCELED.
IT SHOULD NOT. HIPPOLYTA'S DEATH IS A TRAGEDY; HOWEVER, IT HAS NO BEARING ON THE CONTEST.
SO, YOU WOULD RISK CROWNING A MURDERER AS CHAMPION?
THERE ARE MANY SULLIED HANDS ON THIS ISLAND AND IN THIS VERY ROOM. THE POSSIBILITIES OF THAT HAPPENING ARE LIKELY.
THAT'S NOT WHAT I MEANT, AND YOU KNOW THAT.
SEMANTICS.
AND WE CANNOT AFFORD TO GET CAUGHT UP IN SEMANTICS OR MAKE ASSUMPTIONS ABOUT WHO TOOK HIPPOLYTA AWAY FROM US.
HER DEATH IS AN INSURMOUNTABLE LOSS.
PRECISELY WHY THE CONTEST SHOULD BE POSTPONED.

IN MOST CIRCUMSTANCES WE WOULD TAKE THE TIME TO PROPERLY MOURN SUCH A LOSS. BUT THIS IS NOT MOST CIRCUMSTANCES. WE NEED TO ENSURE DOOM'S DOORWAY IS UNDER PROPER WATCH, WHICH REQUIRES A CHAMPION.
THE SAFETY OF NOT ONLY THEMYSCIRA, BUT **THE ENTIRE WORLD,** DEPENDS ON IT.
I CALLED EACH OF YOU HERE SO THAT WE COULD DECIDE DEMOCRATICALLY WHETHER TO MOVE FORWARD WITH THE CONTEST OR NOT.
ALL IN FAVOR OF POSTPONING THE CONTEST, PLEASE SPEAK UP.
THEN IT'S SETTLED.

IF I MAY SPEAK, QUEEN NUBIA?
YES, CASSIE.
I BELIEVE WHOEVER KILLED HIPPOLYTA WOULDN'T ENTER THE CONTEST ANYWAY.
CASSIE IS RIGHT.
WHOEVER DID THIS HAS A DEATH WISH AND THERE ARE MORE THAN ENOUGH INDIVIDUALS CAPABLE OF FULFILLING IT.
PRESENT COMPANY INCLUDED.
AND WE WILL FIND HIPPOLYTA'S MURDERER. BUT IF WE DON'T FIND OUR NEW CHAMPION, WE COULD VERY WELL HAVE ANOTHER CRISIS ON OUR HANDS.

ONE REPRESENTATIVE FROM EACH TRIBE WILL ENTER THE CONTEST. I WILL GIVE TWO DAYS' TIME TO FIGURE OUT WHO THAT WILL BE.
ANY OBJECTIONS?
VERY WELL.
MAY I OFFER TO KEEP INVESTIGATING HIPPOLYTA'S MURDER AS YOU PREPARE FOR THE CONTEST? I BELIEVE I CAN FIGURE OUT WHO GAVE HER THE POISON.
I TRUST YOU ARE THE BEST AMONG US TO FIGURE IT OUT, CASSIE. YOU HAVE MY BLESSING. ALL I ASK IS THAT YOU COME TO ME AS SOON AS YOU HAVE YOUR ANSWERS.
I WILL. HIPPOLYTA CHOSE WELL TO HAVE YOU LEAD IN HER STEAD.

DOOM'S DOORWAY.
WHAT EXACTLY IS BEHIND THIS DOOR THAT REQUIRES SUCH AN EXTREME COMMITMENT? DO THINGS ESCAPE THAT MUCH?
ALTHOUGH THERE HAVEN'T BEEN MANY OCCURRENCES, BREACHES OF THE DOOR HAVE HAPPENED.
I BELIEVE WE'VE ENCOUNTERED SOME OF THEM BEFORE IN MY HOMELAND.
DOOOOOM
WHAT WAS THAT?
MOVEMENT OVER THERE.
ON IT.
THWIP

WAIT A MOMENT.
NYX! YOU ALMOST GOT YOURSELF KILLED.
IS SHE OKAY?
NYX HAS BEEN THROUGH MUCH WORSE.
NUBIA FOUND HER SOME TIME AGO BEHIND DOOM'S DOORWAY. SHE'S A WANDERER, BUT USUALLY KEEPS NEAR HERE.
YOU CAN WRAP HER WOUND WITH THIS.
SHHH... YOU'LL BE OKAY.
I HOPE THIS IS ABOUT AS EVENTFUL AS THINGS GET DOWN HERE.
ME TOO. THE SOONER THE CONTEST STARTS, THE SOONER WE CAN LEAVE.

TRAINING GROUNDS.
THAT WAS A BEAUTIFUL ARRANGEMENT OF FLOWERS, DELPHINE.
THANK YOU. I WAS HONORED TO PUT IT TOGETHER.
ARE WE STILL GOING BY THESMOPHORIA?
I JUST NEED TO CHANGE FIRST.
I'M IN NO RUSH TO GO. TENSION IS ALREADY HIGH ON THE ISLAND, AND SOME ARE JUST ITCHING FOR A REASON TO FIGHT.
DO YOU THINK ANY OF THE AMAZONS FROM THE OTHER TRIBES HAD ANY-THING TO DO WITH THE QUEEN'S DEATH?
THERE IS SURELY NO LOVE LOST BETWEEN BANA-MIGHDALL AND THE THEMYSCIRAN AMAZONS.
THE HISTORY IS A TAD COMPLICATED BETWEEN THE TRIBES.
WHAT ISN'T COMPLICATED AROUND HERE?
HEY!
FWIIIP

WAS THAT AN ARROW?
HELLO, LADIES.
ARE YOU BANA-MIGHDALL OUT OF YOUR MINDS? WHO SHOOTS ARROWS AT THIS TIME OF EVENING?
THOSE WHO WANT TO ALWAYS BE PREPARED NO MATTER THE TIME OF DAY.
IT WAS AN ACCIDENT. A GUST OF WIND CAUGHT THE ARROW.
WE'VE ALREADY HAD ONE TOO MANY FUNERALS TODAY.

CALM DOWN, KARESSI. NOTHING HAPPENED.
I'M FINE.
YOU NEED TO APOLOGIZE TO ANDROMEDA.
IT'S BEEN A LONG DAY. LET'S CALL IT A NIGHT.
KARESSI!
HEY!
PUSH
YOU SHOULD HELP YOUR FRIEND UP AND APOLOGIZE. WE HAVE TRAINING TO FINISH.

APOLOGIZE?
DROP IT.
YOU THINK YOU CAN JUST SHOW UP HERE AND DO AS YOU PLEASE?
I WILL KILL YOU WHERE YOU STAND WITH MY BARE HANDS. I DON'T NEED ANY ERRANT ARROWS TO DO IT FOR ME.
KARESSI! SNAP OUT OF IT!
THAT'S ENOUGH. WHAT HAS GOTTEN INTO YOU? IT'S LIKE YOU BLACKED OUT.
I--I DON'T KNOW. SORRY.

NUBIA'S STUDY.
KNOCK KNOCK
QUEEN NUBIA. IS NOW STILL A GOOD TIME FOR US TO SPEAK? I KNOW WE WERE SUPPOSED TO MEET BUT THEN... HIPPOLYTA.
YES, I KNOW. PLEASE COME IN, MEDUSA.
I WANTED TO ASK YOU ABOUT HOW YOU MANAGED TO LEAVE DOOM'S DOORWAY.
IN ALL THE TIME YOU SPENT GUARDING THE DOOR DID YOU EVER HEAR VOICES CALL OUT TO YOU?
I DID. SOME MORE SINISTER THAN OTHERS.

THE VILEST OF THEM CALLED OUT TO ME. PULLED ME FROM THE END-LESS DARK I WAS IN, OFFERING ME AN ESCAPE.
IT CALLED ITSELF THE APERION.
*APERION?* WHERE HAVE I HEARD THAT BEFORE?
NUBIA, I'M SORRY TO INTERRUPT, BUT--
I SHOULD GO.
DIANA, MY DEEPEST CONDOLENCES.
THANK YOU.

DIANA.
I KNOW WHAT YOU'RE THINKING, BUT I WILL GET THE ANSWERS YOU DESERVE.
AND I WON'T STAND IN YOUR WAY WHEN YOU HAVE THEM.
AND I RESPECT YOU WITH ALL MY BEING, QUEEN.
BUT I CAN'T WAIT A SECOND LONGER.
I INTEND TO USE THE *LASSO OF TRUTH* TO GET ANSWERS NOW.

*Wonder Woman* #785 cover by Travis Moore and Tamra Bonvillain

*Wonder Woman* #785 variant cover by Paulina Ganucheau

DOOM'S DOORWAY.
DOOM
DOOM
...WHAT WAS THAT? IO, YOU HEARD THE NOISE?
YES, AND I DIDN'T LIKE IT.
GODS PROTECT US FROM ANOTHER *CAT.*
SOUNDS LIKE A THREE-VOLLEY SALUTE. I WOULDN'T WORRY ABOUT IT, SISTERS.
THEY MUST BE SENDING HIPPOLYTA OFF. AND WE'RE STUCK DOWN HERE, UNABLE TO OFFER UP EVEN A SINGLE LAMENTATION...
TO GUARD THE DOORWAY IS AN *HONOR.*
INDEED, YARIMA...

"...BUT TRY SAYING THAT WHEN THE PYRE BURNS FOR ONE OF YOUR OWN."
THEMYSCIRAN, ESQUECIDA, AND BANA-MIGHDALL.
THREE AMAZONIAN TRIBES GATHER UNDER THE SAME STARS FOR THE FIRST TIME, AS HIPPOLYTA IS LAID TO REST.
BUT NOT EVERYONE ON THE ISLAND WAS THERE TO PAY TRIBUTE. ONE IN PARTICULAR CAME WITH BAD INTENTIONS...
...AND A VESTED INTEREST IN THE OUTCOME OF THE TRIAL.

EARLIER THAT DAY.
LINE THEM UP!
EVERYONE ON THE ISLAND SHALL BE BOUND BY THE LASSO...
...UNTIL WE HAVE DISCOVERED THE TRUTH ABOUT MY MOTHER'S MURDER!
YOU WOULD QUESTION ME? AS ONE MIGHT AN OUTSIDER?
TOO MUCH TIME IN THE SPHERE OF THE GODS HAS CORRUPTED HER.
A TYPICAL THEMYSCIRAN SOLUTION.
FORGET DIGNITY--USE A DIVINE SHORTCUT AND MENTALLY VIOLATE YOUR SISTERS! WHAT DOES THAT SAY?
IT SAYS THERE IS A KILLER AMONG US.
SISTERS, WITH ALL DUE RESPECT--
WHAT DIANA HAS SUGGESTED IS LOGICAL. I WILL TAKE IT INTO CONSIDERATION...
...BUT ONLY AS A LAST RESORT.
BUT, MY QUEEN, THE LASSO--
I HAVE FAITH THAT THE GUILTY PARTY WILL BE FOUND THROUGH INQUIRY AND INVESTIGATION. THAT IS MY DECISION.
COME, DIANA. WE NEED TO SPEAK.

THE ROYAL PALACE.
NUBIA...I UNDERSTAND YOUR RATIONALE, BUT AN INVESTIGATION WILL ONLY ESCALATE RISING TENSIONS ON THE ISLAND.
WHY HAVE YOU BROUGHT ME TO MY MOTHER'S DEATHBED?
PEACE, DIANA.
WE MEET HERE TO REMIND US OF YOUR MOTHER'S WISDOM.
THIS WRONG, AS GRIEVOUS AS IT IS, CANNOT BE RIGHTED AT THE EXPENSE OF PEACE.
HIPPOLYTA KNEW THE TENUOUS BALANCE BETWEEN OUR TRIBES. EVERYTHING SHE WORKED FOR HANGS ON WHAT WE DO NEXT.
THIS BODY BEFORE YOU...THE BODY OF MY MOTHER!
YOU WOULD SEE HER TO THE FUNERAL PYRE WITHOUT SO MUCH AS A SUSPECT?
THESE THINGS TAKE TIME. IN DEATH, LITTLE IS IDEAL.
THE KILLER WILL BE FOUND AND DEALT WITH.
THIS I SWEAR TO YOU.
YES.
THE KILLER WILL BE DEALT WITH.
I REQUIRE NO PROMISES, FOR I WILL SEE TO IT MYSELF.

LATER, AT THE TEMPLE OF ATHENA.
JUST AS LIFE MUST COME BEFORE DEATH, IT IS UNDERSTOOD THAT THE GODS CAME BEFORE LIFE.
SO IT STANDS TO REASON THAT THE GODS CREATED DEATH **AFTER** THEY CREATED LIFE.
EVER SINCE THAT DAY, THEMYSCIRAN PHILOSOPHERS HAVE LONG DEBATED A SIMPLE QUESTION--
"WHY?"
IT IS TO THIS QUESTION THAT DIANA NOW SEEKS AN ANSWER...

...AND WHO BETTER TO ASK THAN THE GODS THEMSELVES?
GODDESS ATHENA...
I COME BEFORE YOU TODAY NOT AS A PRINCESS, OR AS THE WONDER WOMAN OF THEMYSCIRA...
...BUT AS DIANA, DAUGHTER OF HIPPOLYTA.
MOTHER OF WISDOM, I BOIL IN A CAULDRON OF GRIEF AND RAGE.
SPEAK TO ME. GRANT ME ANSWERS BEFORE THE DOUBT THAT CLOUDS MY THOUGHTS BLINDS ME ENTIRELY.
YOU WON'T GET AN ANSWER.
THE GODS HAVE FALLEN SILENT IN OUR TIME OF STRIFE.
WHO SPEAKS FROM THE SHADOWS?

I AM IN MOURNING, WEARY, AND UNWILLING TO SUFFER THE GAMES OF OTHERS, FRIEND OR FOE.
I HAVE NOT COME HERE FOR MORE QUESTIONS. SHOW YOURSELF!
WHO I AM IS UNIMPORTANT, DIANA. DOOM'S DOORWAY CREAKS AND GROANS-- A GUARDIAN MUST BE NAMED.
WHY HAVE YOU NOT STAKED YOUR CLAIM IN THE TRIAL?
I AM NOT INTERESTED IN COMPETING AGAINST MY SISTERS. THERE ARE OTHERS JUST AS CAPABLE.
WE CONTEND WITH MORE URGENT MATTERS--I AM NEEDED ELSE-WHERE.
ARE YOU?
OR HAS DESIRE USURPED DUTY?
SWOOSH
SAPPHO--!

THIS WAS NOT THE FIRST TIME DIANA HAD BEEN VISITED BY A GHOST, NOR, SHE THOUGHT, WOULD IT BE THE LAST.
SHE PUT LITTLE THOUGHT INTO WHO HAD SPOKEN...
...BUT WHAT IT HAD SAID.
"HAS DESIRE USURPED DUTY?"
THESE WERE WORDS HER MOTHER WOULD HAVE USED.
WHAT DID SHE DESIRE? TO SEE A KILLER BROUGHT TO JUSTICE?
VENGEANCE IS NOT IN HER NATURE, BUT THIS TEMPTATION WAS UNDENIABLE.
HER DUTY, THOUGH, WAS TO FINISH HIPPOLYTA'S WORK. TO SEE THE AMAZONS UNITED.

EACH TRIBE, WITH THEIR OWN CHAMPION...
HOW DOES IT FEEL TO STAND UNDER THE THEMYSCIRAN MOON?
I FEEL AS I ALWAYS HAVE--LIKE AN OUTSIDER.
OURS IS A TRIBE STILL CONTINGENT ON PERMISSION, RATHER THAN THE PROVIDENCE OF THE GODS.
ONE DAY SOON, FARUKA, THINGS WILL CHANGE. YOUR MEMORY OF THIS TIME WILL BE NO CLEARER THAN A DREAM.
A NIGHTMARE, MORE LIKE. WHICH IS WHY THE CHAMPION IN THE TRIAL MUST BE OUR FINEST WARRIOR.
THAT IS WHAT I CAME TO SPEAK TO YOU ABOUT. I WOULD BE HONORED TO SERVE AS CHAMPION--
I KNOW YOU WOULD RELISH THE CHANCE TO REPRESENT THE BANA-MIGHDALL...
...BUT BEFORE YOU COMMIT, I WISH TO PRESENT ANOTHER.
ONE WHO COULD LEAD ANY TRIBE TO VICTORY...
THUNK
...ONE WHO WILL GET INTO THEIR HEADS.
COME, ARTEMIS.

THINK OF HER AS A TACTICAL ADVANTAGE.
BY THE VEIL OF ISIS...
QUEEN FARUKA! I WOULD BE PROUD TO SERVE THE BANA-MIGHDALL, JUST AS I WOULD HELP *ANY* OF MY SISTERS WHO FIND THE ISLAND FORBIDDEN.
I PLEDGE MY SWORD TO YOUR CAUSE OF EQUALITY.
*DONNA TROY* HAS GRACIOUSLY ACCEPTED THE ROLE OF *CHAMPION.* SHE WILL EAT WITH US TONIGHT...
AND TOMORROW WE WILL *TRAIN.*

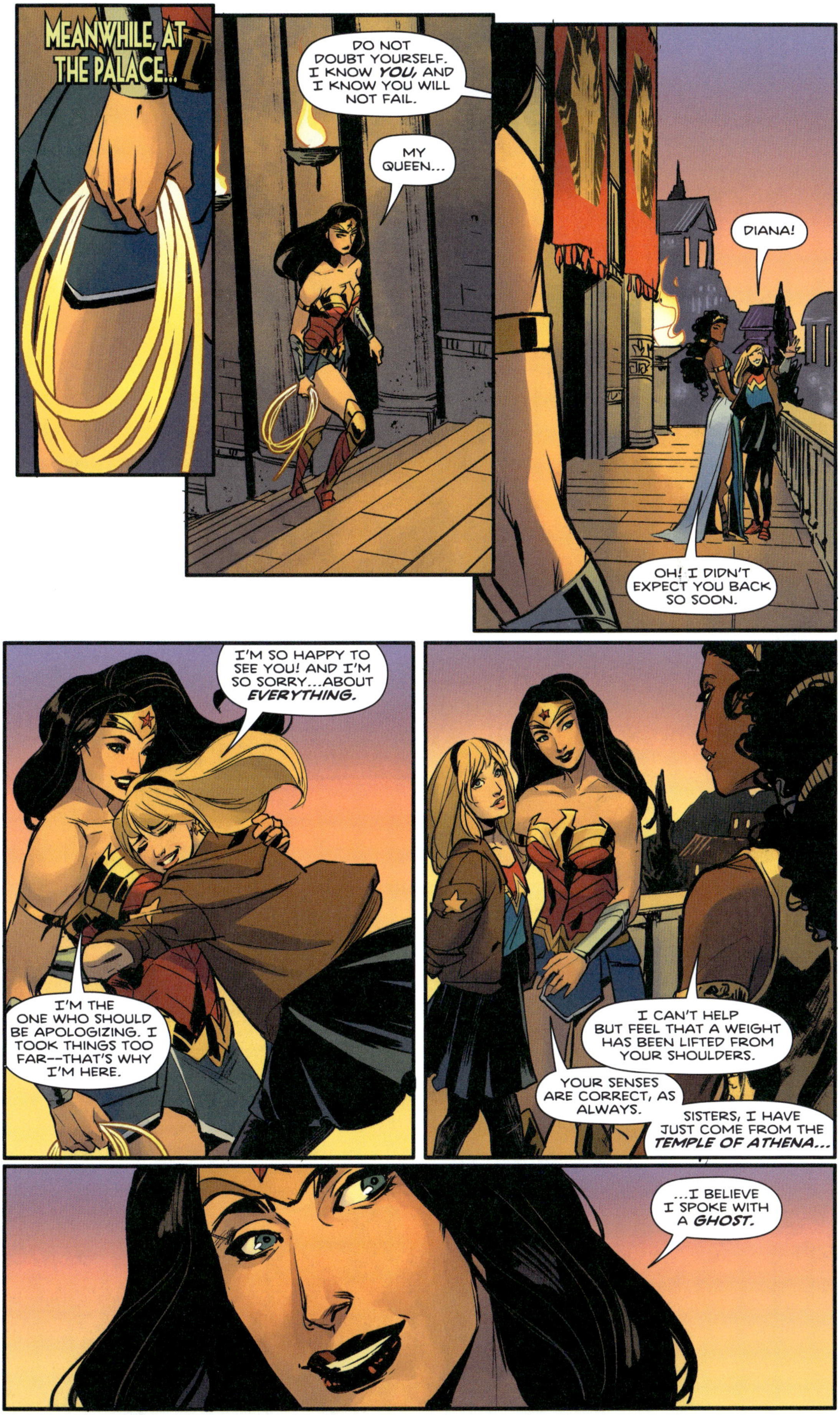
MEANWHILE, AT THE PALACE...
DO NOT DOUBT YOURSELF. I KNOW YOU, AND I KNOW YOU WILL NOT FAIL.
MY QUEEN...
DIANA!
OH! I DIDN'T EXPECT YOU BACK SO SOON.
I'M SO HAPPY TO SEE YOU! AND I'M SO SORRY...ABOUT EVERYTHING.
I'M THE ONE WHO SHOULD BE APOLOGIZING. I TOOK THINGS TOO FAR--THAT'S WHY I'M HERE.
I CAN'T HELP BUT FEEL THAT A WEIGHT HAS BEEN LIFTED FROM YOUR SHOULDERS.
YOUR SENSES ARE CORRECT, AS ALWAYS.
SISTERS, I HAVE JUST COME FROM THE TEMPLE OF ATHENA...
...I BELIEVE I SPOKE WITH A GHOST.

HIPPOLYTA?
AT FIRST I THOUGHT THE SAME THING... BUT MY MOTHER WOULDN'T HAVE SPOKEN FROM THE SHADOWS.
WHAT DID IT SAY?
IT SOMEHOW KNEW MY HEAD AND MY HEART WERE IN DIRECT OPPOSITION. I CANNOT LISTEN TO BOTH.
SINCE I CAN'T PROMISE THAT I WOULDN'T USE IT IN ANGER AGAINST MY SISTERS, AGAINST THE VERY ORDER OF MY QUEEN...
...I SURRENDER THE LASSO OF TRUTH.
YOU PUT THE NEEDS OF THE AMAZONS BEFORE YOUR OWN.
THIS SACRIFICE WILL NOT BE FORGOTTEN.
IT IS ONLY A SACRIFICE IF YOU DO NOT GAIN FROM IT.
I COULDN'T HELP BUT OVERHEAR. DOES GIVING UP YOUR LASSO MEAN YOU'LL BE COMPETING IN THE TRIAL?
IT MEANS I LISTENED TO THE ADVICE OF MY SISTERS, ATALANTA. NOTHING MORE, NOTHING LESS.
THE BANA-MIGHDALL HAVE CHOSEN THEIR CHAMPION, AND SOON THE ESQUECIDA WILL TOO.
YOU'LL HAVE TO CHOOSE A SIDE SOONER OR LATER, NIECE...

"...WE *ALL* WILL."
EVERY WOMAN MUST DRINK FROM THE BOWL.
THEN, OUT OF MANY WILL COME *ONE.*
WHAT VISIONS DO YOU SEE, ANAHI?
DRINK, AND I WILL *TELL* YOU.
I SEE THE SPIRIT OF OUR ESQUECIDA...
...STRONG, SILENT. WAITING IN DARKNESS.
...I SEE *YOU*, YARA.
I SEE THE FUTURE OF OUR PEOPLE...
I SEE THE LONG ROAD WE HAVE TRAVELED, AND THE HIDDEN PATH AHEAD.
AND ON THAT PATH...

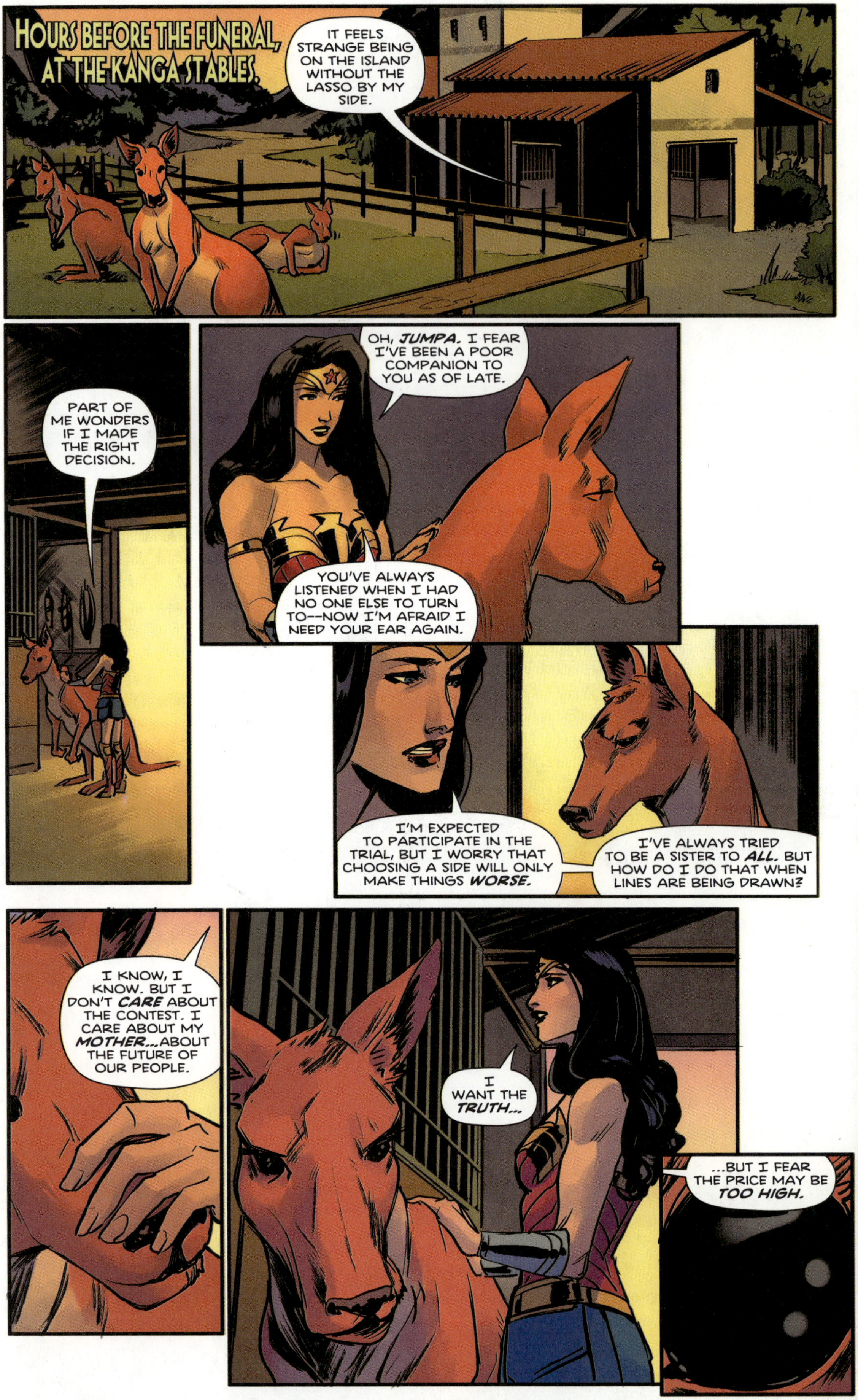
HOURS BEFORE THE FUNERAL, AT THE KANGA STABLES.
IT FEELS STRANGE BEING ON THE ISLAND WITHOUT THE LASSO BY MY SIDE.
PART OF ME WONDERS IF I MADE THE RIGHT DECISION.
OH, JUMPA. I FEAR I'VE BEEN A POOR COMPANION TO YOU AS OF LATE.
YOU'VE ALWAYS LISTENED WHEN I HAD NO ONE ELSE TO TURN TO--NOW I'M AFRAID I NEED YOUR EAR AGAIN.
I'M EXPECTED TO PARTICIPATE IN THE TRIAL, BUT I WORRY THAT CHOOSING A SIDE WILL ONLY MAKE THINGS WORSE.
I'VE ALWAYS TRIED TO BE A SISTER TO ALL. BUT HOW DO I DO THAT WHEN LINES ARE BEING DRAWN?
I KNOW, I KNOW. BUT I DON'T CARE ABOUT THE CONTEST. I CARE ABOUT MY MOTHER... ABOUT THE FUTURE OF OUR PEOPLE.
I WANT THE TRUTH...
...BUT I FEAR THE PRICE MAY BE TOO HIGH.

DOOM'S DOORWAY.
RUMMMMBLE
THAT NOISE! RHEA, YARIMA--DID YOU HEAR IT?
THAT WAS NO RIFLE...
IT CAME FROM BEHIND THE *DOOR.*
DOOOOMM
WHATEVER COMES THROUGH... STAND YOUR GROUND.

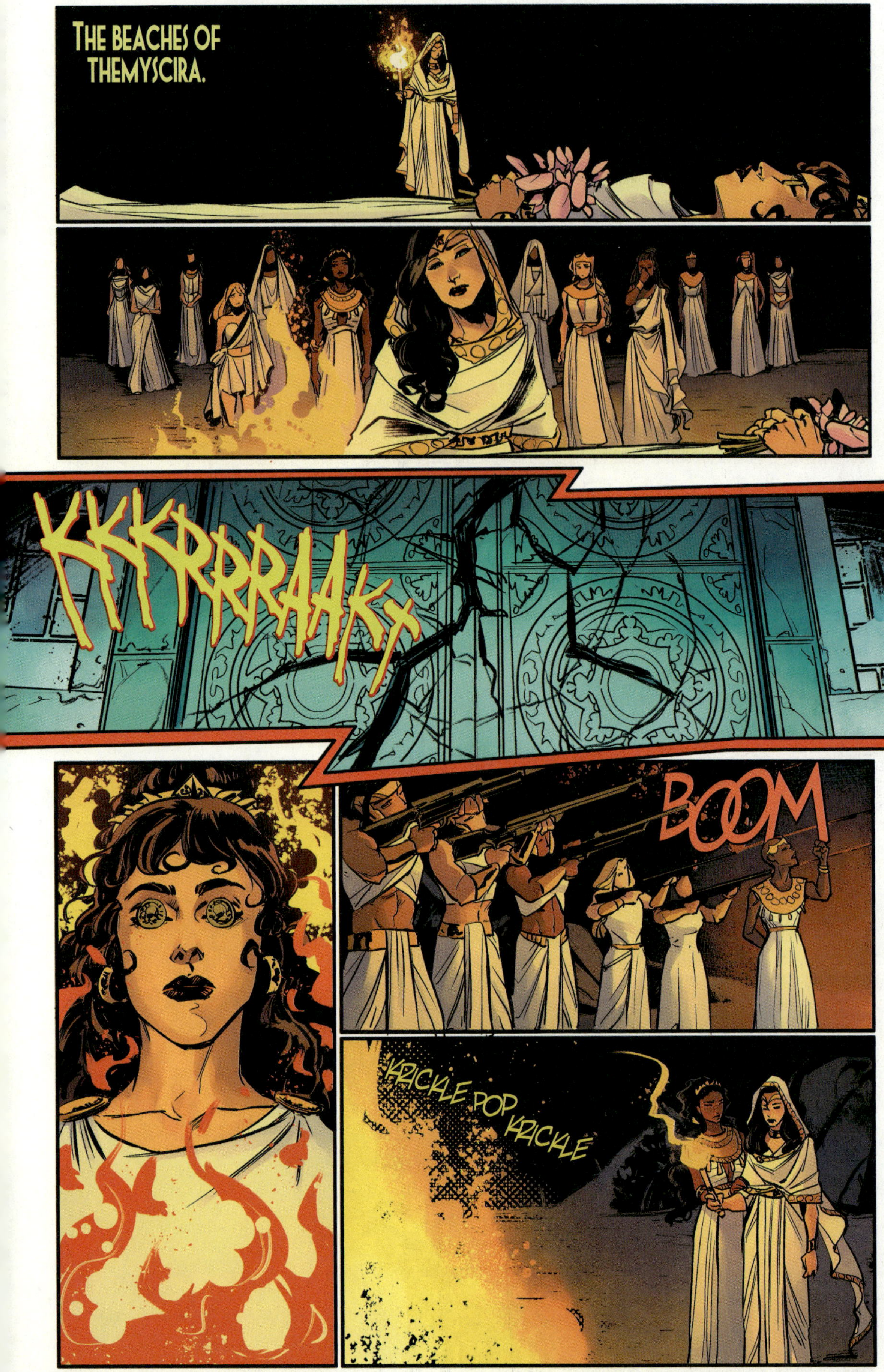
THE BEACHES OF THEMYSCIRA.
KKKRRRAAKK
BOOM
KRICKLE POP KRICKLE

WHAT THE HELL IS BEYOND THAT DOOR?
WHAT WICKED MAGIC IS THIS?
PUSH IT BACK, YARIMA! PUSH IT BACK!
I CAN'T--THIS POISON...IT'S IN MYYY--
YAAARRGHH!
BOOM
URRAAAGHH...
AMUN-RA, I CALL TO YOU IN MY DISTRESS...
BOOM
DOOM
KRAK-THOOM

THE FOLLOWING MORNING...
THIS IS A FOUL OMEN.
YARIMA AND RHEA WERE FOUND DEAD IN FRONT OF DOOM'S DOORWAY.
I'M TOLD IO WILL RECOVER FROM HER WOUNDS, BUT IT WILL TAKE TIME. SHE REMAINS UNCONSCIOUS.
IO...
I'M SORRY MY QUEEN, BUT IT IS FOR HER SAKE WE MUST ACT SOON.
WHAT WILL BECOME OF THEMYSCIRA IF WE DON'T ELECT A CHAMPION? QUEEN HIPPOLYTA WOULD HAVE--
PHILIPPUS, I KNOW YOU ARE HURTING, AND I'M QUITE AWARE OF THE URGENCY.
BUT SHOWING WEAKNESS WILL ONLY THREATEN OUR PARADISE. IT IS PRECISELY FOR IO THAT I HOLD MYSELF TOGETHER.
BUT WE WILL NEED TIME TO PREPARE--
THEN I WILL ELECT A CHAMPION WHO REQUIRES NO PREPARATION.
A TRUE LION NEED NOT STRETCH BEFORE LUNGING AT ITS PREY. NOW PLEASE...
I NEED A MOMENT TO MYSELF.
I THOUGHT PERHAPS DIANA WOULD COMPETE ON THEMYSCIRA'S BEHALF, BUT I FEAR GRIEF CONSUMES HER...AS IT THREATENS TO CONSUME US ALL.
WITHOUT YOUR GUIDANCE AS QUEEN, THE TRIBES WILL FALL INTO CHAOS.
WE CANNOT RISK FURTHER STRIFE.
GIVE ME TIME TO THINK.

"UNEASY LIES THE HEAD THAT WEARS A CROWN."
NUBIA IS TROUBLED THAT A WRITER FROM MAN'S WORLD CAPTURED HER EMOTIONS SO PERFECTLY IN A SINGLE LINE.
SHE IS NOT TROUBLED, HOWEVER, BY THE CHOICE THAT LIES BEFORE HER...
FOR SHE HAS **ALREADY** MADE IT.
AS QUEEN, NUBIA SWORE AN OATH TO PROTECT HER SISTERS--**ALL** HER SISTERS.
A PROMISE THAT, WITH EVERY PASSING HOUR, BECOMES MORE AND MORE DIFFICULT TO KEEP...

...THOUGH NOT IMPOSSIBLE. NOT YET, AT LEAST.
THEMYSCIRANS, BANA-MIGHDALL, ESQUECIDA--AMAZONS ALL, MY SISTERS.
I WELCOME YOU TO THE PALACE ATRIUM, WHERE OUR THREE TRIBES GATHER FOR THE FIRST TIME ON THE SAME SOIL.
WE MEET NOW TO AFFIRM OUR PACT, FORMALLY ENDORSE THE TERMS OF THIS TRIAL, AND PROCLAIM THE CHAMPIONS OF OUR TRIBES!
QUEEN FARUKA WILL PRESENT OUR PREDETERMINED AGREEMENT.
THANK YOU, NUBIA.
IT HAS BEEN DETERMINED THAT ALL WEAPONS NOT INCLUDED IN THE GAMES WILL BE CONFISCATED AND SEALED IN THE ARMORY, WHERE THEY WILL BE HELD UNTIL THE CONCLUSION OF THE CONTEST.
THE DISCOVERY OF UNAUTHORIZED ARMS ON NON-SECURITY DETAIL WILL BE MET WITH EXTREME PREJUDICE.
THESE ARE THE TERMS AGREED UPON BY ALL, TO MAINTAIN A BALANCED FIELD WHEN THE TRIAL BEGINS.
THAT MEANS NO GOLDEN EAGLE ARMOR OR SANDALS OF HERMES TO GAIN THE UPPER HAND...
THE TRIAL WILL BE FAIR.
SO LET US REVEAL OUR CHAMPIONS.

OUR TRIBE, HIDDEN FOR THESE MANY YEARS-- THE ESQUECIDA, WHOSE CHAMPION HAS BEEN FORESEEN. WE OFFER FORTH...
...YARA FLOR.
AS QUEEN OF THE THEMYSCIRANS, I PRESENT OUR CHAMPION--
PHILIPPUS. CAPTAIN OF THE GUARD, AND QUEEN HIPPOLYTA'S GENERAL.
MY QUEEN--!
...IT WOULD BE AN HONOR.
AND NOW WE, THE BANA-MIGHDALL, ARE PROUD TO PRESENT OUR CHAMPION.
DONN--
HOLD!

I, DIANA, DAUGHTER OF HIPPOLYTA, THROW IN MY GAUNTLET TO COMPETE IN THE TRIAL!
I AM BEHOLDEN TO NONE...
...A CHAMPION FOR *NO* TRIBE, BUT FOR *ALL* AMAZONS!
TRIAL OF THE AMAZONS PART 3
MICHAEL W. CONRAD AND BECKY CLOONAN WRITERS ROSI KÄMPE ARTIST TAMRA BONVILLAIN COLORIST
PAT BROSSEAU LETTERER TRAVIS MOORE AND TAMRA BONVILLAIN COVER PAULINA GANUCHEAU VARIANT COVER
NICOLA SCOTT AND ANNETTE KWOK INTERNATIONAL WOMEN'S DAY VARIANT COVER CHRIS ROSA ASSOCIATE EDITOR
BRITTANY HOLZHERR EDITOR PAUL KAMINSKI SENIOR EDITOR WONDER WOMAN CREATED BY WILLIAM MOULTON MARSTON

*Trial of the Amazons: Wonder Girl* #1 cover by Joëlle Jones and Jordie Bellaire

*Trial of the Amazons: Wonder Girl* #1 variant cover by Jeff Dékal

Themyscira.
THE ESQUECIDA'S ARRIVAL, MERE HOURS BEFORE THE DEATH OF HIPPOLYTA.
I HATE THE GODS.
SPECIFICALLY, I HATE THE GODS OF OLYMPUS.
THEY SIT ON HIGH AND MEDDLE IN THE AFFAIRS OF HUMANITY TO HELP THEM PASS THE ENDLESS ETERNITY IN FRONT OF THEM.
RAPE, MURDER, SICKNESS, GREED... YACHT ROCK.
NONE OF THESE WOULD EXIST HAD THEY NOT DECIDED IT TO BE SO.
AND HERE I AM, FACING THEM ONCE AGAIN.
WONDERING TO MYSELF WHY THE THEMYSCIRANS, SUCH POWERFUL WOMEN...
ARE THEY SUCH SLAVES TO THE PAST THEY CAN'T SEE HOW POWERFUL THEY ARE WITHOUT THEM?
...WOULD BOW DOWN AND SERVE THOSE MEGALOMANIACS LIVING IN GILDED PALACES NOT GIVING A CRAP ABOUT THEM?

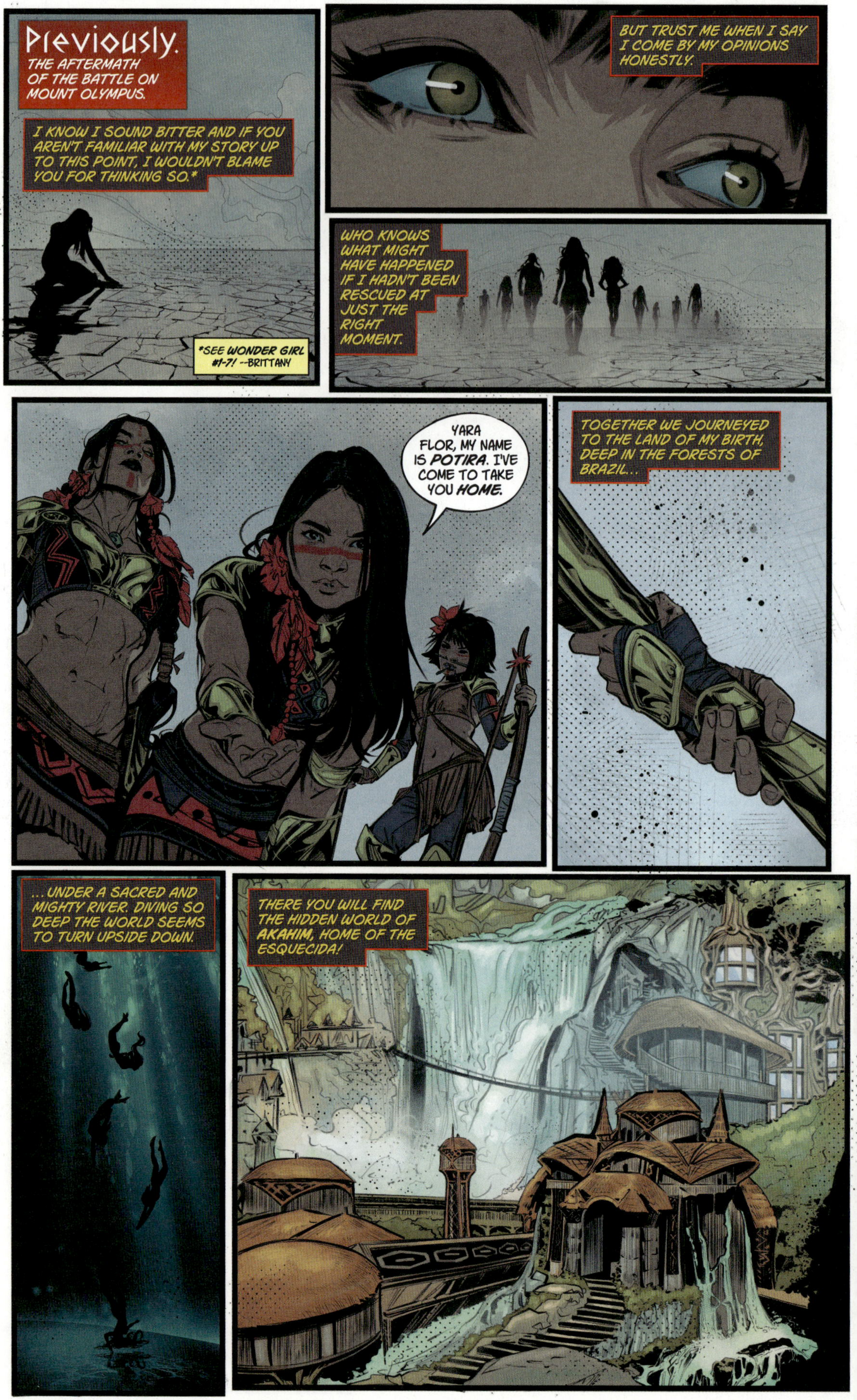
Previously.
THE AFTERMATH OF THE BATTLE ON MOUNT OLYMPUS.
I KNOW I SOUND BITTER AND IF YOU AREN'T FAMILIAR WITH MY STORY UP TO THIS POINT, I WOULDN'T BLAME YOU FOR THINKING SO.*
*SEE WONDER GIRL #1-7! --BRITTANY
BUT TRUST ME WHEN I SAY I COME BY MY OPINIONS HONESTLY.
WHO KNOWS WHAT MIGHT HAVE HAPPENED IF I HADN'T BEEN RESCUED AT JUST THE RIGHT MOMENT.
YARA FLOR, MY NAME IS POTIRA. I'VE COME TO TAKE YOU HOME.
TOGETHER WE JOURNEYED TO THE LAND OF MY BIRTH, DEEP IN THE FORESTS OF BRAZIL...
...UNDER A SACRED AND MIGHTY RIVER. DIVING SO DEEP THE WORLD SEEMS TO TURN UPSIDE DOWN.
THERE YOU WILL FIND THE HIDDEN WORLD OF AKAHIM, HOME OF THE ESQUECIDA!

THEY HAVE GONE BY MANY NAMES AND THE STORIES OF THEIR BEGINNINGS DIFFER, BUT SOME SAY THAT IT CAME AS A WHISPER CARRIED ON THE WIND BY GAIA TO THE MOON GODDESS YACY. INSPIRED THEN, AND DRAWING UPON THE WELL, SHE CREATED THESE DIVINE WOMEN OF THE SACRED WATERS.
WEARING NECKLACES OF JADE AMULETS, THEY MAINTAIN THEIR MATRIARCHAL SOCIETY THROUGH SACRED RITUAL.
THEY WOULD DEDICATE THEIR LIVES TO PROTECTING THE LAND AND PRESERVING THE BALANCE OF NATURE...
...IN TIME BECOMING SOLDIERS OF LEGEND AND INSPIRING COUNTLESS AROUND THE WORLD WITH THEIR EXAMPLE!
THIS IS WHERE MY STORY BEGINS...

THEY TOOK ME IN WITH OPEN ARMS, GIVING ME THE LOVE AND ACCEPTANCE NEEDED TO CLAIM MY BIRTHRIGHT AND EARN A PLACE BESIDE THEM.
POTIRA

I THOUGHT I HAD BEEN TAUGHT ALL THERE WAS TO KNOW ABOUT THE ART OF COMBAT FROM CHIRON ON OLYMPUS, BUT I WAS SO WRONG!
THESE WOMEN! THESE GREAT WARRIORS FOUGHT IN WAYS PASSIONATE AND INTUITIVE, EVERYONE GIVEN ROOM FOR EXPRESSION YET ALL GROUNDED IN THE ART OF DISCIPLINE TO MAKE IT POSSIBLE.
WE FOUGHT SIDE BY SIDE LIKE FORCES OF NATURE AND LIFE BEGAN TO TAKE ON A SHAPE THAT ALMOST BECAME FAMILIAR...

UNTIL ONE DAY, IT NO LONGER WAS.
IT STARTED WITH THE ANIMALS...
RAMPAGING AND STUPID, IT DESTROYED EVERYTHING IN ITS PATH.
...TAKING DOWN THE SLOBBERING ALIEN PIG AND WINNING THE DAY!

...AND THEN SLOWLY THE POISON SPREAD TO THE VERY LANDSCAPE AROUND US.
AND THEN ONE DAY, IT FINALLY SHOWED ITSELF. NOT ITS TRUE FACE, SOMETHING MORE LIKE A SYMPTOM...
TOGETHER WE FACED MANY THREATS, BUT THEY FELT THIS WAS NOT OF THEIR WORLD.
BUT I KNEW EXACTLY WHERE IT HAD COME FROM...
ONLY THE GODS OF OLYMPUS WOULD BE SO CRUEL AS TO INTERFERE WITH MY LIFE NOW.
WHATEVER THEY INTENDED, THE ESQUECIDA PROVED THEY WERE WORTHY OF THE CHALLENGE...
BUT GODS OR NO GODS THE DAY WAS NOT WITHOUT ITS LOSSES. IT SEEMED MY NEXT LESSON WAS ABOUT MOURNING THE DEAD.
I WANTED TO TAKE IT ALL TO HEART, TO HONOR THEIR MEMORIES AND SACRIFICE...
...BUT I WAS ONLY CONSUMED WITH REVENGE!

AT THE SAME TIME, THE QUEEN GABOYMILA GATHERED A JURY TO DISCUSS WHAT IT COULD ALL MEAN.
EVERYBODY QUIET! QUIET DOWN! ANAHI WISHES TO SPEAK TO US OF HER VISION!
I ALWAYS LIKED ANAHI BUT NOTHING SHE EVER SAID MADE A LICK OF SENSE!
AND I WASN'T THE ONLY ONE WHO THOUGHT SO, APPARENTLY.
WHY?
HOW ARE WE TO JOURNEY TO SUCH A PLACE?
DO THEY MEAN US HARM?
IS THIS THE CAUSE OF THE BLACK ROT IN THE FOREST?
HOW COULD WE NOT HAVE KNOWN OF THEM?
WHERE?
MY SISTERS...
...WE MUST GO TO THIS ANCIENT ISLAND ANAHI SPEAKS OF. IT IS THE HOME OF OUR DISTANT COUSINS, THE THEMYSCIRANS, TASKED WITH GUARDING THE DOOR THAT HOLDS IN THE VERY CREATURES OF HELL!
OUR SACRED PROMISE TO PROTECT THESE LANDS MUST BE KEPT!

I MYSELF CANNOT GO. THE ILLNESS IN MY BODY PREVENTS SUCH A JOURNEY.
THEREFORE, IT SHALL FALL TO YOU, POTIRA, TO ACT AS QUEEN IN MY PLACE.
GATHER THOSE YOU THINK MOST WORTHY AND WISE AND LEAD THEM ON THIS MISSION.
ME?
OH...
...AND TAKE OUR NEWEST SCOUT YARA WITH YOU.
SHE SHARES BLOOD WITH THEM AND COULD ACT AS AN IMPORTANT CONNECTION FOR US.
SHE COULD BE AN IMPORTANT CONNECTION FOR US TO THE OUTSIDE WORLD, DON'T YOU THINK?
!!!
Y-YES?
ASSEMBLE YOUR TEAM AND LEAVE FOR THEMYSCIRA AT FIRST LIGHT...
"...FOR THE IMBALANCE OF NATURE AND NEGLECT OF DUTY SHALL NOT GO UNPUNISHED."

Themyscira.
THE NIGHT OF HIPPOLYTA'S FUNERAL PYRE.
OF ALL THESE WOMEN, WHO COULD HAVE POSSIBLY WANTED HIPPOLYTA DEAD?
QUEEN NUBIA WILL BE WANTING ANSWERS SOON--
--AND YET I CANNOT IMAGINE ANY OF HER SISTERS, NEW OR ESTRANGED, HATING HER ENOUGH TO POISON HER.

WHAT ABOUT FARUKA? SHE HATES THE THEMYSCIRANS MORE THAN ANYBODY. SHE RAGES AGAINST THE INJUSTICES COMMITTED BY THEM IN THE PAST AND HAS MADE HER VENGEANCE WELL KNOWN.
SHE ALSO HAS THE MOST TO GAIN IF HIPPOLYTA WAS SUDDENLY OUT OF THE WAY...
...BUT USING A WEAPON LIKE POISON AND CREEPING ABOUT IN THE SHADOWS LIKE A COWARD? IT JUST SIMPLY ISN'T HER STYLE.
NO.
NOT FARUKA.
HOW ABOUT ATALANTA? SHE'S ONE OF THE OLDEST AMAZONS AND MAY THINK IT'S FINALLY HER TIME TO ASSUME THE THRONE.
ARTEMIS?
NO, NO WAY! I KNOW HER, AND I REFUSE TO BELIEVE--BUT--

--NO! WE ARE FRIENDS, I WOULD KNOW IF--
BUT--
HEY, ARTEMIS! WAIT UP!
WHAT IS IT, CASSIE?
I JUST WANTED TO ASK YOU A FEW QUESTIONS--
ABOUT WHAT?
WELL NUBIA THOUGHT IT MIGHT BE A GOOD IDEA TO HAVE ME INVESTIGATE HIPPOLYTA'S MURDER AND I THOUGHT MAYBE YOU--

MAYBE I WHAT? WHAT ARE YOU ASKING ME?!
ALL RIGHT...
...DID YOU POISON HIPPOLYTA?
NUBIA MUST HAVE LOST ALL SENSE WHEN CHOOSING *YOU* FOR THIS TASK. OUT OF RESPECT FOR OUR PAST FRIENDSHIP I WILL ALLOW THIS INSULT TO STAND, BUT ASK ME THAT *AGAIN*...
...AND IT WILL BE THE LAST SENTENCE YOU *UTTER*.
SHE REMEMBERS I'M *HALF GOD*, RIGHT?
YOU KNOW, THREATS LIKE THAT AREN'T REALLY HELPING YOUR CASE!

Themyscira.
SHORTLY AFTER THE ESQUECIDAS' ARRIVAL AND THE FINAL PEACEFUL HOURS BEFORE THE DEATH OF HIPPOLYTA.
POTIRA PROVED TO BE A GREAT CHOICE AS LEADER BUT SHE ALSO RECOGNIZED OUR NEED TO EXPLORE AND BLOW OFF A LITTLE STEAM WITH OUR LONG-LOST "COUSINS" THE THEMYSCIRANS AND BANA-MIGHDALL.
ONLY I COULDN'T HELP BUT THINK OF ALL THE YEARS I SPENT GROWING UP ALONE.
HERE I WAS POSITIVELY SURROUNDED BY A BRAND NEW FAMILY, BUT I FELT LONELIER THAN EVER.
TAVERN OF THESMOPHORIA
SOMEONE WAS MISSING.
THE ONLY THREAD THAT COULD TIE THESE WORLDS TOGETHER... MY MOTHER, AELLA, WAS GONE.

HER ABSENCE FROM THE MOMENTOUS EVENTS HAPPENING AROUND ME HAD NEVER FELT SO PAINFULLY CLEAR UNTIL NOW.
Later.
THE FEAST OF THE GATHERED TRIBES. TWO HOURS BEFORE THE DEATH OF HIPPOLYTA.
SMACK SMACK
GOOD CHICKEN!
WHAT WAS THAT, MY DEAR?
AHEM
SORRY, YOUR MAJESTY, I MEAN... THIS CHICKEN IS... UH... A... NOSHINGLY PLEASANT REPAST FOR MY... UH... BELLY?
OH MY GOD! SO EMBARRASSING!
THAT'S ALL RIGHT, THERE IS NO NEED TO BE SO FORMAL. I HAVE HEARD IT SAID THAT ONE CAN ONLY TRULY UNDERSTAND A CULTURE THROUGH ITS FOOD. I LOOK FORWARD TO LEARNING MORE ABOUT YOURS.
WELL, I'M SORT OF RELEARNING IT MYSELF, BUT I BELIEVE THEY ALSO ENJOY CHICKEN, HIGHNESS.

YOU KNOW, I KNEW YOUR MOTHER, AELLA, BEFORE SHE LEFT THEMYSCIRA.
REALLY, YOU DID?!
SHE WAS A FIERCE AND PASSIONATE WOMAN. HEADSTRONG AT TIMES BUT THERE WASN'T A WARRIOR ON EARTH YOU WOULD RATHER HAVE FIGHTING BY YOUR SIDE.
SHE WOULD BE MOST PROUD OF THE WOMAN YOU HAVE BECOME.
...I...
NO ONE KNEW HIPPOLYTA WOULD BE DEAD BY MORNING AND THIS WAS THE LAST TIME MANY OF US WOULD SEE HER.
IT IS MY PLEASURE, YARA FLOR.

Days later.
MY INVESTIGATION HADN'T THUS FAR YIELDED ANY DEFINITIVE LEADS...
SNIFF SNIFF
BUT I WAS ABLE TO ANALYZE THE EVIDENCE AND GATHER MY POOL OF POTENTIAL SUSPECTS...
I INTERVIEWED PRACTICALLY EVERYONE PRESENT ON THE ISLAND AND EVEN SOME WHO WEREN'T PRESENT BUT WHO HAD THE MEANS TO INTERFERE.
ANYONE WITH AN AXE TO GRIND OR SOMETHING TO GAIN FROM HIPPOLYTA'S DEATH.
#2
Leave Meeting
I TRIED MY BEST TO BE DELICATE DUE TO THE CIRCUMSTANCES...
YOU KILLED HER! DIDN'T YOU?!
...BUT MY EFFORTS WERE GETTING ME NOWHERE.
SO, I DID WHAT ANY GOOD DETECTIVE WOULD...
I RETRACED MY STEPS BACK TO THE BEGINNING TO SEE IF THERE WAS SOMETHING I MISSED.
AND THAT IS WHEN I FOUND IT.
OH! IT WAS--

Doom's Doorway.
AAHH!
Themyscira.
THE ARMORY.
Kanga Stables.
SCHH-SLINK

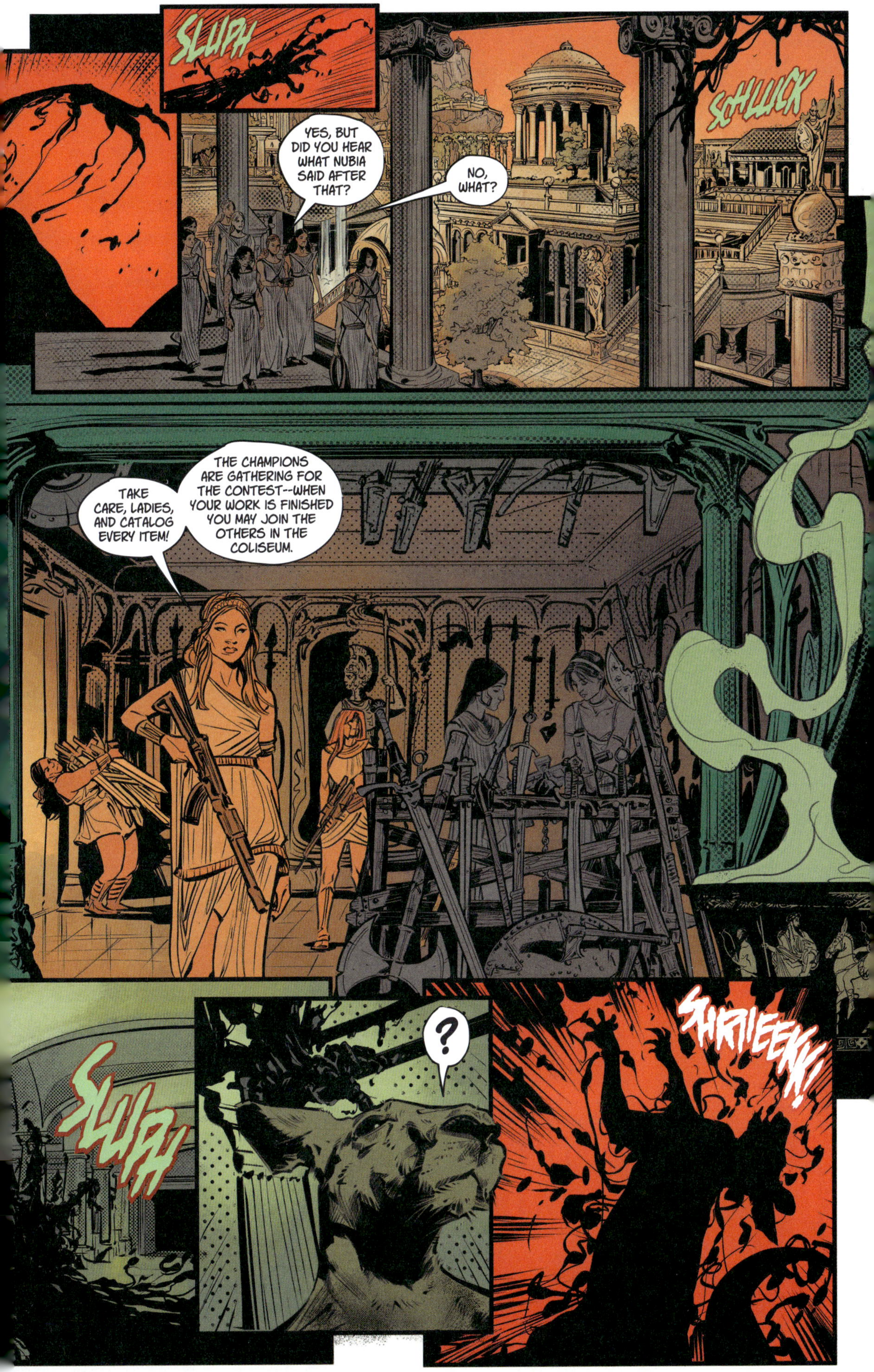

SLUPH
YES, BUT DID YOU HEAR WHAT NUBIA SAID AFTER THAT?
NO, WHAT?
SCHLUCK
TAKE CARE, LADIES, AND CATALOG EVERY ITEM!
THE CHAMPIONS ARE GATHERING FOR THE CONTEST--WHEN YOUR WORK IS FINISHED YOU MAY JOIN THE OTHERS IN THE COLISEUM.
SLUPH
?
SHRIEEKK!

EACH TRIBE WITH ITS OWN CHAMPION. ONE BY ONE THEY STEP FORWARD TO TAKE PART IN THE CONTEST.
THE BANA-MIGHDALL PRESENT DONNA TROY.
THE ESQUECIDA OFFER FORTH YARA FLOR.
THE THEMYSCIRANS PRESENT PHILIPPUS, CAPTAIN OF THE GUARD AND QUEEN HIPPOLYTA'S GENERAL.
DIANA, DAUGHTER OF HIPPOLYTA, BEHOLDEN TO NONE, COMPETES FOR ALL AMAZONS!
TRIAL OF THE AMAZONS PART 4
JOËLLE JONES SCRIPT & ART JORDIE BELLAIRE COLORIST PAT BROSSEAU LETTERER
JONES AND BELLAIRE COVER JEFF DEKAL VARIANT COVER JILLIAN GRANT ASSISTANT EDITOR BRITTANY HOLZHERR EDITOR
PAUL KAMINSKI SENIOR EDITOR WONDER WOMAN CREATED BY WILLIAM MOULTON MARSTON

*Wonder Woman* #786 cover by Travis Moore and Tamra Bonvillain

*Wonder Woman* #786 variant cover by Paulina Ganucheau

AS THE SUN RISES OVER THEMYSCIRA.
FROM EACH TRIBE, A CHAMPION--AND FROM EACH PATRON GODDESS, A DEED THROUGH WHICH THEY WILL PROVE THEIR WORTH.
THOUGH THE TASKS ARE YET UNKNOWN, THE CHOSEN WILL BE GIVEN A TOOL TO AID THEM IN THE CONTEST... BUT KNOW THIS: EACH ITEM CAN BE USED BUT ONCE.
THE GODS DEMAND THAT THE FEATS MUST BE ACCOMPLISHED BEFORE THE CONTEST'S END. ONLY THEN WILL A VICTOR BE CROWNED.
THESE CUSTOMS MUST BE OBSERVED, LEST THE RESULTS BE CORRUPTED.
SINCE THE DAWN OF OUR TRIBE, THE HUNT HAS DEFINED THE ESQUECIDA. TODAY WE HUNT NOT JUST FOR SURVIVAL, BUT FOR A LONG-LOST SISTERHOOD.
TO OUR CHAMPION, YARA FLOR, WE GIVE A BOW AND ARROW.
FOR TOO LONG THE BANA-MIGHDALL HAVE FACED THEIR OWN PERPLEXING QUESTION: WHY MUST WE FIGHT FOR EQUALITY?
AND SO THE BANA-MIGHDALL OFFER THEIR CHAMPION, DONNA TROY, A KNOTTED LARIAT, IN ORDER TO SOLVE THE PUZZLE.
THE CHAMPION OF THEMYSCIRA SHALL RECEIVE THE COMPASS. LONG HAS IT BEEN OUR GUIDE ACROSS LAND AND OVER SEA, THROUGH LIFE, AND INTO THE GREAT BEYOND.
PHILIPPUS, MAY THIS COMPASS HELP YOU NAVIGATE THE PATH AHEAD.
WE THANK OUR ORACLES, ANAHI, OLABISI AND PENELOPE. SO THE GODS HAVE SPOKEN. STEP FORTH, CHAMPIONS. TAKE YOUR PLACES IN THE ARENA.
AND AS FOR YOU, DIANA...

...YOUR MANY SACRIFICES HAVE EARNED YOU A PLACE IN THE TRIAL, INDEPENDENT OF ANY TRIBE.
THANK YOU, MY QUEEN.
TELL US. WHAT WILL YOU BRING?
I WILL CARRY A SWORD. A WEAPON OF WAR, COURAGE, AND JUSTICE. YET IT REPRESENTS PEACE THROUGH STRENGTH, AND BATTLE AS A LAST RESORT.
THIS WAS ALWAYS THE NATURE OF MY MISSION AS WONDER WOMAN IN MAN'S WORLD, AND REMAINS SO--EVEN NOW.
VERY WELL.
WHEN THE CONTEST BEGINS, THERE CAN BE NO STOPPING IT. SUCH IS THE WILL OF THE GODS.
SHE WHO COMPLETES EACH TASK, WHILE EXEMPLIFYING AMAZON VALUES, SHALL BE DEEMED BY PROVIDENCE TO BE THE VICTOR.
THE FUTURE OF ALL AMAZONS HANGS IN THE BALANCE.
MAY THE MOST WORTHY AMONG YOU WIN.
HURRAH! YAH!
YAAAAH!

HURRAH! YAH! YAAAAH!
MY BROTHERS AND SISTERS, LONG HAVE YOU WAITED IN DARKNESS. AS I HAVE PROMISED, YOUR PATIENCE SHALL BE REWARDED!
THE HOUR WE HAVE ANTICIPATED HAS FINALLY COME. THE RECKONING IS AT HAND!
MY SIBLINGS...
IT IS TIME TO AWAKEN THE MOTHER.
I ALMOST HOPE SOME OF YOU AMAZONS LIVE...
...IF ONLY TO CURSE THE NAME OF HE WHO BROUGHT ABOUT YOUR UNDOING.
ALTUUM.
THE SURVIVOR.
HWOOOO
HWOOOO
RUMMBL
RUMMBL
SKSHH

SHATHOOM
WHERE ARE THEY? POTIRA, FARUKA, DID YOU SEE WHAT HAPPENED?
*COUGH* NO! *COUGH COUGH* WAS THAT--
BY THE RISEN OSIRIS...
THEY'RE GONE!
NO!

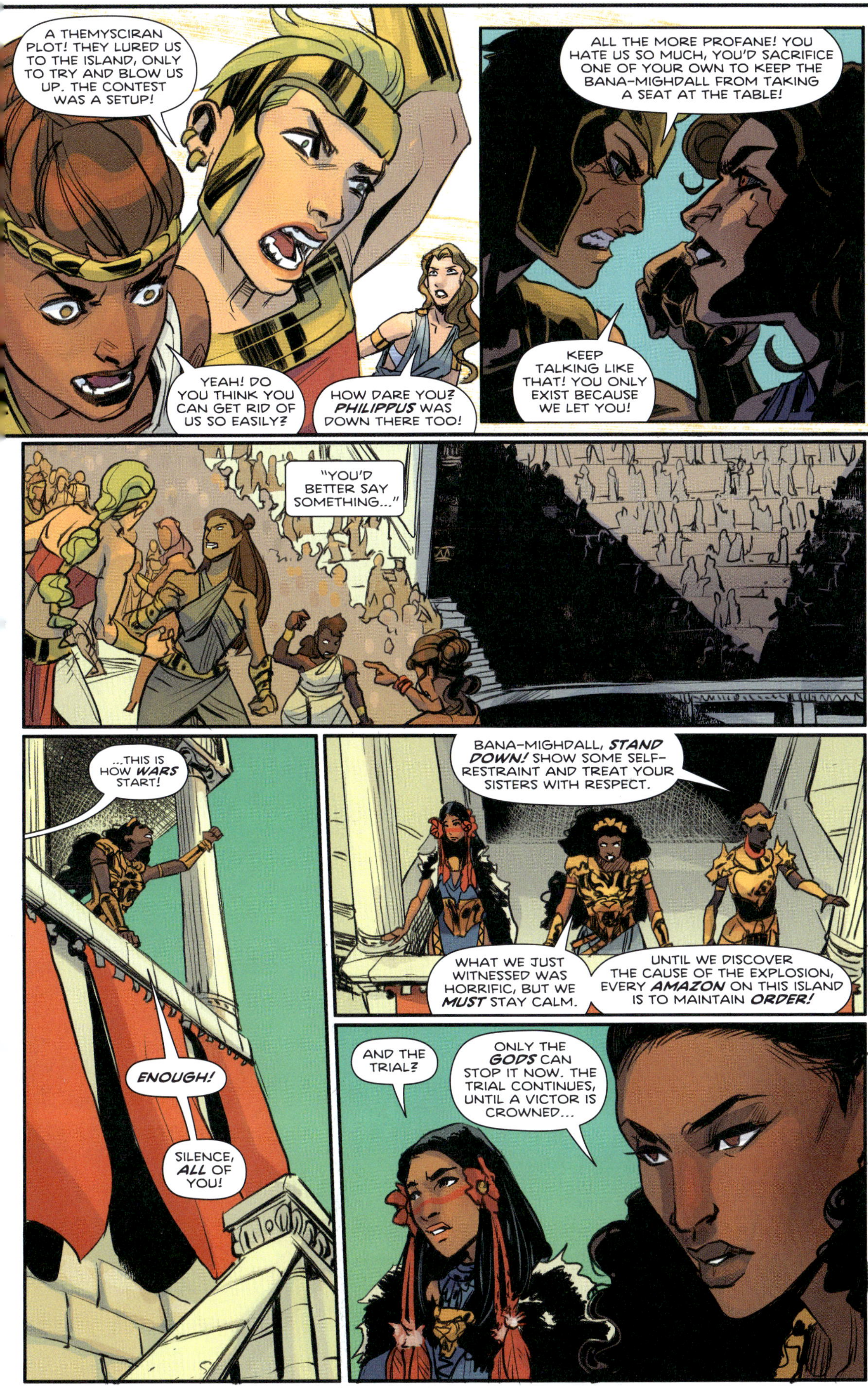

A THEMYSCIRAN PLOT! THEY LURED US TO THE ISLAND, ONLY TO TRY AND BLOW US UP. THE CONTEST WAS A SETUP!
YEAH! DO YOU THINK YOU CAN GET RID OF US SO EASILY?
HOW DARE YOU? PHILIPPUS WAS DOWN THERE TOO!
ALL THE MORE PROFANE! YOU HATE US SO MUCH, YOU'D SACRIFICE ONE OF YOUR OWN TO KEEP THE BANA-MIGHDALL FROM TAKING A SEAT AT THE TABLE!
KEEP TALKING LIKE THAT! YOU ONLY EXIST BECAUSE WE LET YOU!
"YOU'D BETTER SAY SOMETHING..."
...THIS IS HOW WARS START!
ENOUGH!
SILENCE, ALL OF YOU!
BANA-MIGHDALL, STAND DOWN! SHOW SOME SELF-RESTRAINT AND TREAT YOUR SISTERS WITH RESPECT.
WHAT WE JUST WITNESSED WAS HORRIFIC, BUT WE MUST STAY CALM.
UNTIL WE DISCOVER THE CAUSE OF THE EXPLOSION, EVERY AMAZON ON THIS ISLAND IS TO MAINTAIN ORDER!
AND THE TRIAL?
ONLY THE GODS CAN STOP IT NOW. THE TRIAL CONTINUES, UNTIL A VICTOR IS CROWNED...

"...OR UNTIL WE KNOW FOR CERTAIN IF OUR CHAMPIONS ARE DEAD."
DONNA, ARE YOU ALL RIGHT?
I WAS CAUGHT BY SURPRISE, THAT'S ALL.
YOU DON'T HAVE TO START CODDLING ME NOW, DIANA.
WHERE... WHERE ARE WE?
MY GUESS IS *UNDER* THE ARENA. WE MUST HAVE FALLEN DEEP UNDER-GROUND.
THOUGH I'VE NEVER HEARD MENTION OF THESE TUNNELS BEFORE.
NOR HAVE I, AND HESTIA KNOWS I SPENT MY YOUTH EXPLORING EVERY HIDDEN CAVERN ON THIS ISLE.
THAT EXPLOSION--DO YOU THINK WHATEVER CAUSED IT...
OR *WHO*EVER...
CHANCES ARE IT'S STILL DOWN HERE. STAY ON YOUR GUARD.
UGH, THIS ROPE IS USELESS WITH ALL THESE KNOTS!
HERE...
PUSH IT TOGETHER, THEN LOOP IT AROUND...
WHY HELP ME? ISN'T THIS SUPPOSED TO BE A *CONTEST?*
YES.
AND *TOGETHER* WE JUST MIGHT SURVIVE IT.

CLANK
THIS CAVE... IT DOESN'T LOOK NATURAL.
YOU'RE RIGHT. IT MUST HAVE BEEN CONSTRUCTED BEFORE THE ARENA.
SAPPHO WEPT! IMAGINE IF THESE TUNNELS PREDATE THEMYSCIRA ITSELF--
QUIET, SISTERS. DO YOU HEAR THAT?
WE'RE NOT ALONE.
THE WALLS--THEY'RE COVERED...
SKSHHHHH
CLANK
RHEIA PRESERVE US. THIS ISN'T A CAVE...
...IT'S A *TOMB!*

WE COULDN'T HAVE FALLEN THAT FAR.
LET'S GET BACK TO THE SURFACE--THIS ISN'T WHAT WE SIGNED UP FOR.
I WON'T GIVE UP ON THE CONTEST. THE BANA-MIGHDALL PUT THEIR FAITH IN ME, I'M NOT GOING TO AND LET THEM DOWN.
WAIT. WE WERE TO PERFORM CERTAIN FEATS, CORRECT? DONNA, WHAT DID THE ORACLE SAY YOURS WAS?
I THINK MY CHALLENGE WAS TO BE A PUZZLE.
AND YOU, PHILIPPUS. WHAT DID PENELOPE TELL YOU?
NAVIGATION... WHICH COULD POSSIBLY MEAN FINDING OUR WAY OUT OF THIS LABYRINTH.
AND, YARA... WHEN I SEE A BOW, IT ONLY MEANS ONE THING.
A HUNT.
THAT NOISE--COULD IT BE OUR QUARRY?
GODS. WHAT IF WE HAVE IT ALL WRONG?
SKISHHHHHH
WHAT DO YOU MEAN?
WHAT IF WE ARE THE PREY?
SKISHHHHHH
CLANK

IF THAT IS THE CASE, THEN WE NEED TO KEEP MOVING.
PHILIPPUS, PERHAPS NOW IS THE TIME TO USE THE *COMPASS.*
TELL IT TO LEAD US TO THE SURFACE!
*WHAT?* NO! ASK WHERE WE SHOULD GO TO COMPLETE THE CONTEST!
GODDESS ATHENA, IN YOUR WISDOM...
...SHOW US THE WAY TO WHAT WE NEED TO FIND.
HOLA! IT WORKS!
THAT WAS PRETTY COOL. IT'LL BE INTERESTING TO FIND OUT EXACTLY WHAT THAT COMPASS THINKS WE *NEED.*
TRIAL OR NO, IN THIS LABYRINTH THERE IS NO ROOM FOR RIVALRIES.
FROM HERE ON OUT, WE COMPETE *TOGETHER.*
YOU'RE RIGHT. WE'RE HERE AS AMAZONS, EQUAL AND UNITED.
I GET IT-- THE CONTEST'S IMPORTANT TO ME TOO, I GUESS. MY TRIBE CAME SO FAR JUST TO *BE* HERE, AND HONESTLY?
I DON'T WANNA LET THEM DOWN.
EVERY ASPECT OF THE TRIAL IS SANCTIFIED BY THE GODS--NOT JUST OF ONE PANTHEON, BUT OF *ALL THREE.*
IF IT IS BY THEIR WILL THAT WE WERE SENT TO THESE CATACOMBS, THEN LET US ENDEAVOR AS A TEAM.

THIS DIDN'T FEEL LIKE AN EXPLOSION TO ME. FOR ONE, I DIDN'T HEAR A DETONATION.
I AGREE. I'VE SEEN SINKHOLES LIKE THIS BEFORE--IT LOOKS LIKE A CAVE-IN.
THAT WOULD SUGGEST A CAVERN UNDER THE ARENA, BUT I KNOW OF NO SUCH THING.
IF WE CLEAR SOME OF THIS RUBBLE OUT, WE CAN SEND A TEAM IN AFTER THEM.
HAVE FAITH, NUBIA. WE SENT OUR BEST TO THE CONTEST--IT WILL TAKE MORE THAN A SIMPLE FALL TO KILL THEM.
STILL...WE HAVE NO IDEA WHAT COULD BE DOWN THERE.
LOOK OUT!
THWAK
WHAT IN HADES?!
QUEEN NUBIA! SOMETHING'S WRONG WITH THEM--NOBODY WILL LISTEN TO REASON!
MENA, IRACI! HELP HER!
HANG ON, CASSIE!
EASY NOW, I GOT YOU.

OLABISI, PENELOPE, ANAHI! ARE ANY OF YOU HURT?
WE ARE UNHARMED, MY QUEEN...BUT I'M AFRAID WE WON'T REMAIN SO FOR LONG.
THEIR MINDS ARE UNDER ATTACK. A POWERFUL FORCE--I'VE NEVER FELT ITS EQUAL.
YOU ARE THE MOST CAPABLE ORACLES THE AMAZONS HAVE EVER KNOWN. THERE MUST BE SOMETHING YOU CAN DO TO CALM THEM?
I DON'T KNOW. IT'S SO STRONG...
THERE'S NO HARM IN TRYING, THOUGH. COME ON.
WE CAN'T *HNNGH* HOLD IT BACK FOR LONG...
BUT WE CAN BUY YOU SOME TIME.
WHATEVER YOU'RE DOING, IT'S WORKING!
WE NEED TO GET DOWN THERE--I'VE GOT SOMETHING TO TELL THE QUEEN.
I'D STAKE MY LIFE THAT WHATEVER IS CAUSING THIS MADNESS IS COMING THROUGH DOOM'S DOORWAY.
IT'S NOT COMING THROUGH-- IT'S ALREADY HERE.

MEANWHILE, DOWN IN THE CATACOMBS...
LOOKS LIKE THE END OF THE ROAD. DOES ANY OF THIS LOOK FAMILIAR TO YOU?
NO. I'M STILL SHOCKED THIS OSSUARY EVEN EXISTS.
I WONDER WHO ALL THESE PEOPLE WERE? THIS IS THEIR FINAL RESTING PLACE, BUT WHERE DID THEY COME FROM...
...AND HOW DID THEY DIE?
DON'T LOOK NOW, BUT WE'VE GOT COMPANY.
...THE GROSS KIND.
IT'S TOO DARK--I CAN'T SEE WHERE THEY'RE COMING FROM!
SCHLUK
I THINK WE FOUND WHAT HAPPENED TO ALL THESE PEOPLE. EATEN BY GIANT *UNGH* BUGS!
FSSK
PHILIPPUS, WILL YOU BE ALL RIGHT WITHOUT A WEAPON?
HAH! I TRAINED DIANA. I THINK I'LL MANAGE.
BUT WHY DID THE COMPASS LEAD US TO A DEAD END?
SCHLLLUK
NO. NOT A DEAD END...
...BUT A TEMPLE.

AND YOU SHALL BE A FITTING SACRIFICE FOR ECHIDNA!
WHOOSH
HOUNDS OF HADES!
NOT TODAY!
KRASH
UGH, THAT SMELL! WHAT IS THIS THING?
SLASH
THE ROTTING ONE! BORN FROM THE FETID SWAMPS OF TARTARUS--SHE IS THE MOTHER OF ALL MONSTERS!
MY MOTHER, HIPPOLYTA, BEHEADED YOU, OR DON'T YOU REMEMBER?
A FEAT I SHALL GLADLY REENACT, IN HER HONOR!
KE KE KE KEEE!
CUT OFF MY HEAD, I SHALL JUST GROW ANOTHER!

SHE MIGHT BE RIGHT! WHAT IF WE CAN'T KILL HER?
CRUSH
THEN WE WILL BIND HER. SEE THESE CHAINS?
HNNGH! SHE WAS IMPRISONED HERE BEFORE!
FOOLS!
THUNKK
OUFF!
HISSS! YOU CANNOT CONTAIN ME, AMAZON!
AMAZONS.
THERE ARE FOUR OF US.

TELL US, POISONOUS LAMPREY. WHY ATTACK NOW? WHO SET YOU FREE?
YESSS, I WASTED AWAY, IMPRISONED IN THESE FORGOTTEN DEPTHS...UNTIL I HEARD THE SOUND.
THE SOUND OF A HORN MADE FROM MY OWN OFFSPRING, THE CHIMERA! ITS CALL GAVE ME THE STRENGTH TO SHATTER MY OWN BONDS!
ONCE I FINISH WITH YOU, I SHALL RETURN TO THE SURFACE! KE KE KE KEEE!
MY CHILDREN WILL COVER YOUR ISLAND, THEN SPREAD LIKE A GLORIOUS SCOURGE ACROSS THE EARTH!
SORRY, BUT THAT SOUNDS LIKE A TERRIBLE PLAN.
SWOOSH
I KNOW YOU--TROIA, THE DARKSTAR!
YOU CAN CALL ME DONNA.
KER-RASH

WHOA!
SCRTCHHH
I'VE GOT YOU, NOW LET GO OF THE ROPE!
NO! YOU HEARD THE CREATURE! WE CAN'T LET IT ESCAPE--
YARA, I WISH WE COULD HAVE MET UNDER LESS DIRE CIRCUMSTANCES.
I TOTALLY GET IT. AND I'M WITH YOU...
...LET'S GO KILL THAT THING.

YOU CAN'T HOLD ME ANY LONGER! I WILL NOT BE KEPT FROM MY OFFSPRING!
RHEA, GIVE ME STRENGTH!
SKRASH
LOOK THERE, BEHIND THE MONSTER...I KNOW WHERE WE ARE!
SHE BROUGHT US TO *DOOM'S DOORWAY!*
--AND TO HER OWN DEMISE! *HOLA!*
FWIP

SSSSKREEE!
SPLUK
HURK!
I WILL NOT DIE! YOU WILL NOT SEE ME BEATEN!
PERHAPS NOT--BUT THERE IS ALWAYS ANOTHER WAY!
DONNA, HOLD THE ROPE! YARA, PHILIPPUS-- OPEN THE DOOR!
OPEN THE-- ARE YOU SURE?!
GO! DO AS DIANA SAYS!
KREAAAK
ALL RIGHT-- NOW WHAT?!

NOW WE PUSH HER THROUGH!
NO! I WILL NOT BE--KHHHAAA! MY CHILDREN...
MY CHILDREN!
Diana...
You promised me redemption.
UNGH... NO...
YOU LIED!
CHAOS...

DIANA, YOU BLACKED OUT FOR A SECOND. ARE YOU--
UNGH.
RUMMMBL
THIS ROOM'S COLLAPSING!
SCREW THE GODS, I'M OFFICIALLY *ENDING* THIS CONTEST. WE HAVE TO GET OUT OF HERE, *NOW!*
RUMMMBL
UNFF!
I'M ALL RIGHT. *GO!* PHILIPPUS, YOU KNOW THE WAY OUT FROM HERE!
I DO. FOLLOW ME!
I'M NOT LEAVING YOU BEHIND!
COME ON! WE CAN'T STAY HERE!
NO! *DIANA!*
TELL THEM--TELL NUBIA--
IT'S *CHAOS!*

COUGH COUGH
KER-KER-RAK
STOP IT--LET ME GO!
AAGGGGH!
SHE WILL ENDURE. THAT'S DIANA DOWN THERE, REMEMBER? IF ANYONE CAN SURVIVE A COLLAPSE...
I KNOW. I JUST WISH I COULD HAVE DONE MORE.
NOTHING WENT HOW I HOPED IT WOULD.
WHEN DOES IT EVER? COME ON. DIANA GAVE US A MESSAGE.
YOU'RE RIGHT. WE NEED TO DELIVER IT...

"CHAOS HAS COME TO THEMYSCIRA!
"NONE AMONG US WILL BE SAFE!"
TRIAL OF THE AMAZONS PART 5
MICHAEL W. CONRAD AND BECKY CLOONAN WRITERS ROSI KÄMPE AND BECKY CLOONAN ARTISTS
MARISSA LOUISE COLORIST PAT BROSSEAU LETTERER TRAVIS MOORE AND TAMRA BONVILLAIN COVER
PAULINA GANUCHEAU VARIANT COVER CHRIS ROSA ASSOCIATE EDITOR BRITTANY HOLZHERR EDITOR
PAUL KAMINSKI GROUP EDITOR WONDER WOMAN CREATED BY WILLIAM MOULTON MARSTON

*Trial of the Amazons: Wonder Girl #2* cover by Joëlle Jones and Jordie Bellaire

*Trial of the Amazons: Wonder Girl #2 variant cover by Babs Tarr*

THEMYSCIRA

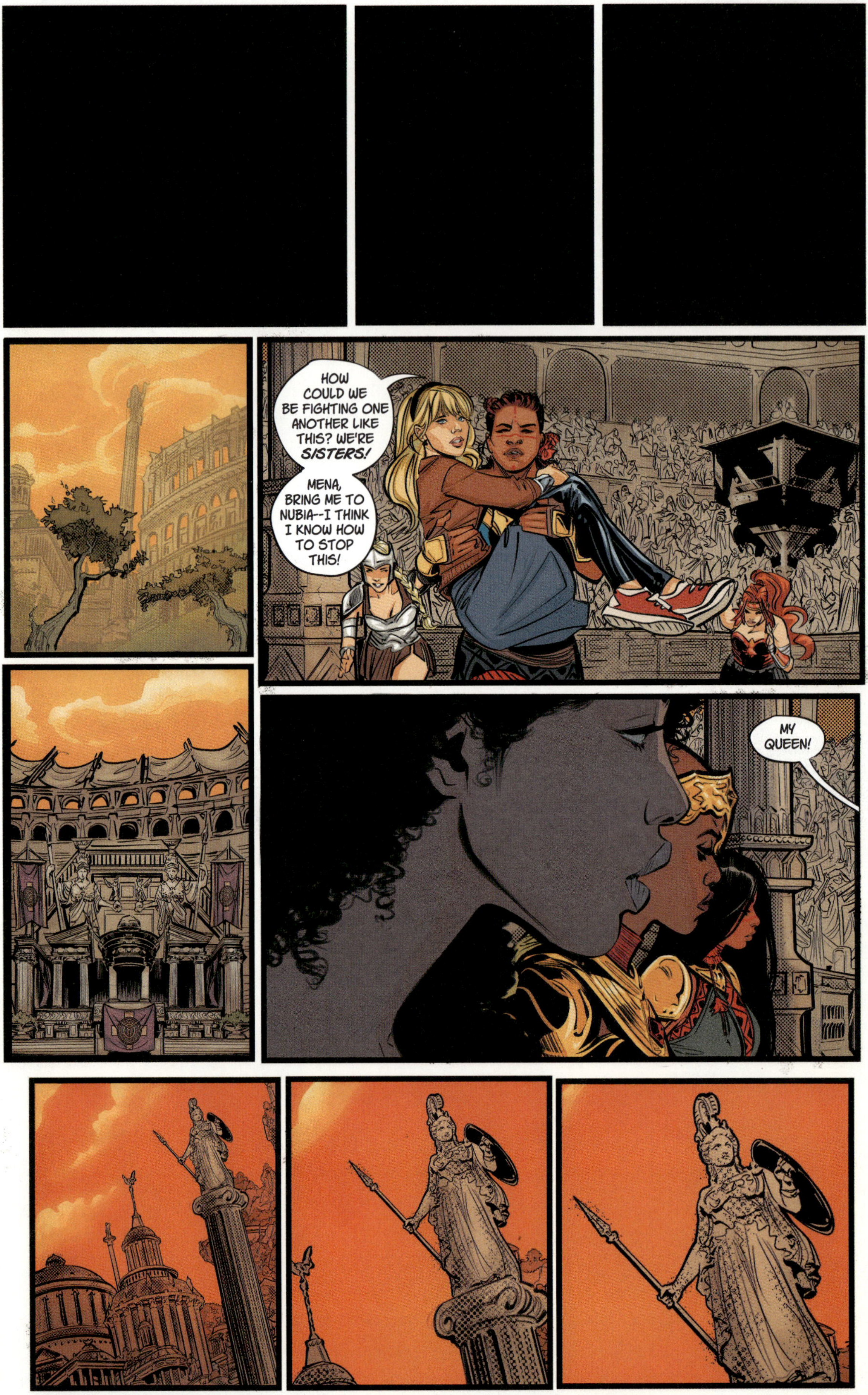
HOW COULD WE BE FIGHTING ONE ANOTHER LIKE THIS? WE'RE *SISTERS!*
MENA, BRING ME TO NUBIA--I THINK I KNOW HOW TO STOP THIS!
MY QUEEN!

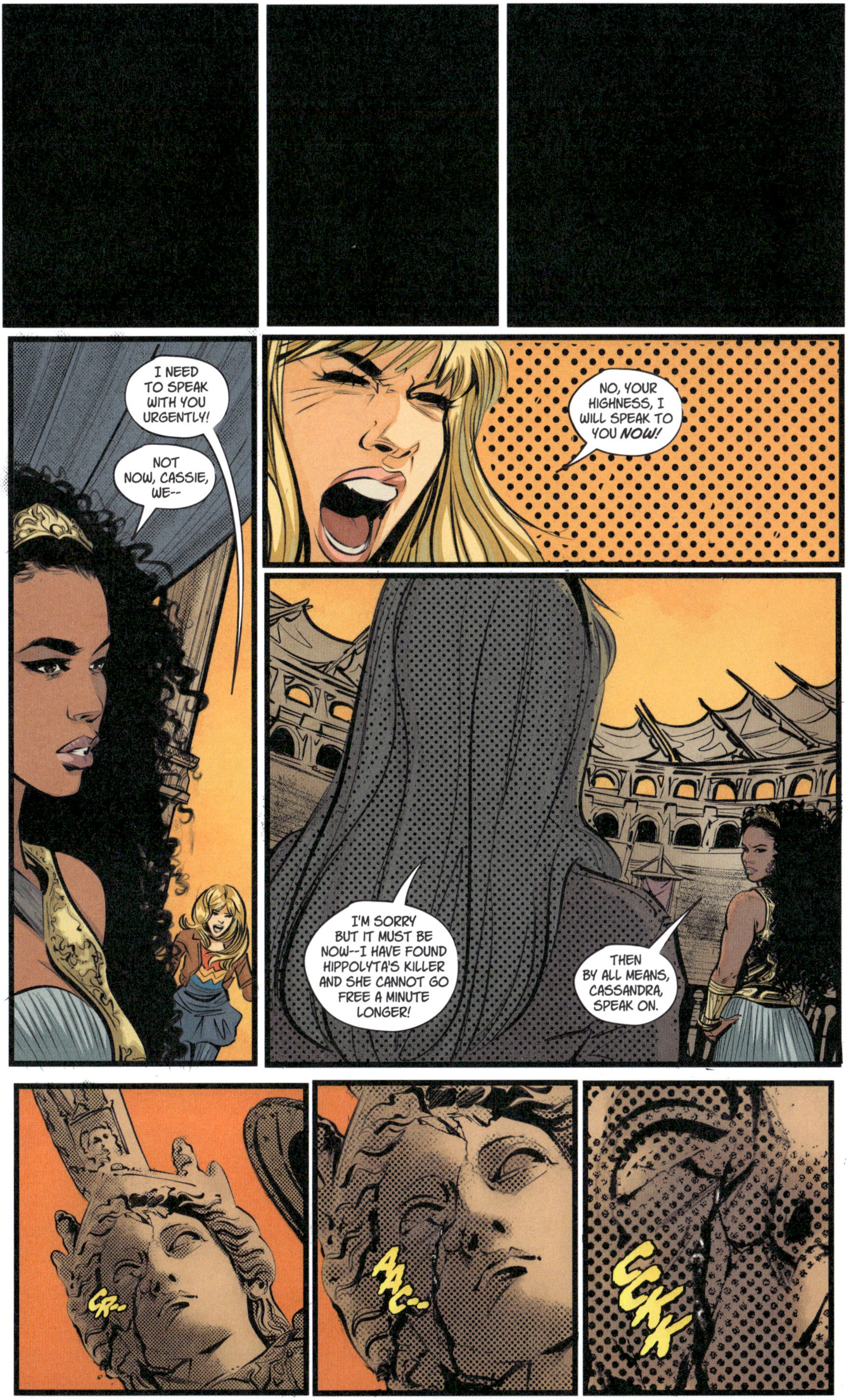
I NEED TO SPEAK WITH YOU URGENTLY!
NOT NOW, CASSIE, WE--
NO, YOUR HIGHNESS, I WILL SPEAK TO YOU *NOW!*
I'M SORRY BUT IT MUST BE NOW--I HAVE FOUND HIPPOLYTA'S KILLER AND SHE CANNOT GO FREE A MINUTE LONGER!
THEN BY ALL MEANS, CASSANDRA, SPEAK ON.
CR--
AAC--
CCKK

WELL, BUCKLE UP! BECAUSE I'M GOING TO NOT ONLY REVEAL WHO HIPPOLYTA'S MURDERER IS, BUT I WILL TAKE YOU STEP BY STEP TO ABSOLVE THOSE WHOM I HAVE SUSPECTED OF KILLING HER.
SO AS TO REMOVE ANY DOUBT THAT ONLY ONE OF YOU COULD HAVE DONE IT!
GO ON.
I THINK SHE IS PLAYACTING AS DETECTIVE NOW.
WHAT'S HAPPENING?
OH GODS!
"ASSUMING THE MURDER TOOK PLACE DURING THE FEAST OF THE TRIBES SOMETIME AFTER HIPPOLYTA LEFT AND BEFORE NUBIA DISCOVERED HER BODY...LET US WALK THROUGH THE EVENTS, STARTING AT--
The Hall of Celebration,
PALACE OF THEMYSCIRA. TWO HOURS BEFORE THE DEATH OF HIPPOLYTA.
"POTIRA, MENA, YARA, HIPPOLYTA, DIANA, ATALANTA, ARTEMIS, AND FARUKA, YOU WERE ALL SEATED ON THE DAIS--I KNOW BECAUSE I WAS SITTING FRONT AND CENTER WITH THE ESQUECIDA AND HAD A CLEAR VANTAGE POINT TO EVERYTHING THAT WOULD HAPPEN THERE THAT EVENING.

"QUEEN NUBIA STOOD AND ADDRESSED THE ASSEMBLY...
WE ARE GOING TO HAVE A CONTEST, IT'S GOT RULES, BUT THEY WON'T MATTER 'CAUSE THE GODS WILL INTERFERE, LIKE ALWAYS, SO--
"THEN FARUKA RUDELY INTERRUPTED--"
INTERRUPTED?! I WAS MERELY POINTING OUT THE PRIVILEGED--
SURE, OKAY, BUT STILL, YOU INTERRUPTED THE SPEECH...
"...I EVEN TALKED ABOUT IT WITH DONNA AND IRACI.
"NEXT THING I KNOW WHEN I LOOKED BACK UP THERE, HIPPOLYTA AND PHILIPPUS WERE SAYING THEIR FAREWELLS.
"THIS LEADS ME TO MY FIRST SUSPECT, *PHILIPPUS.*"

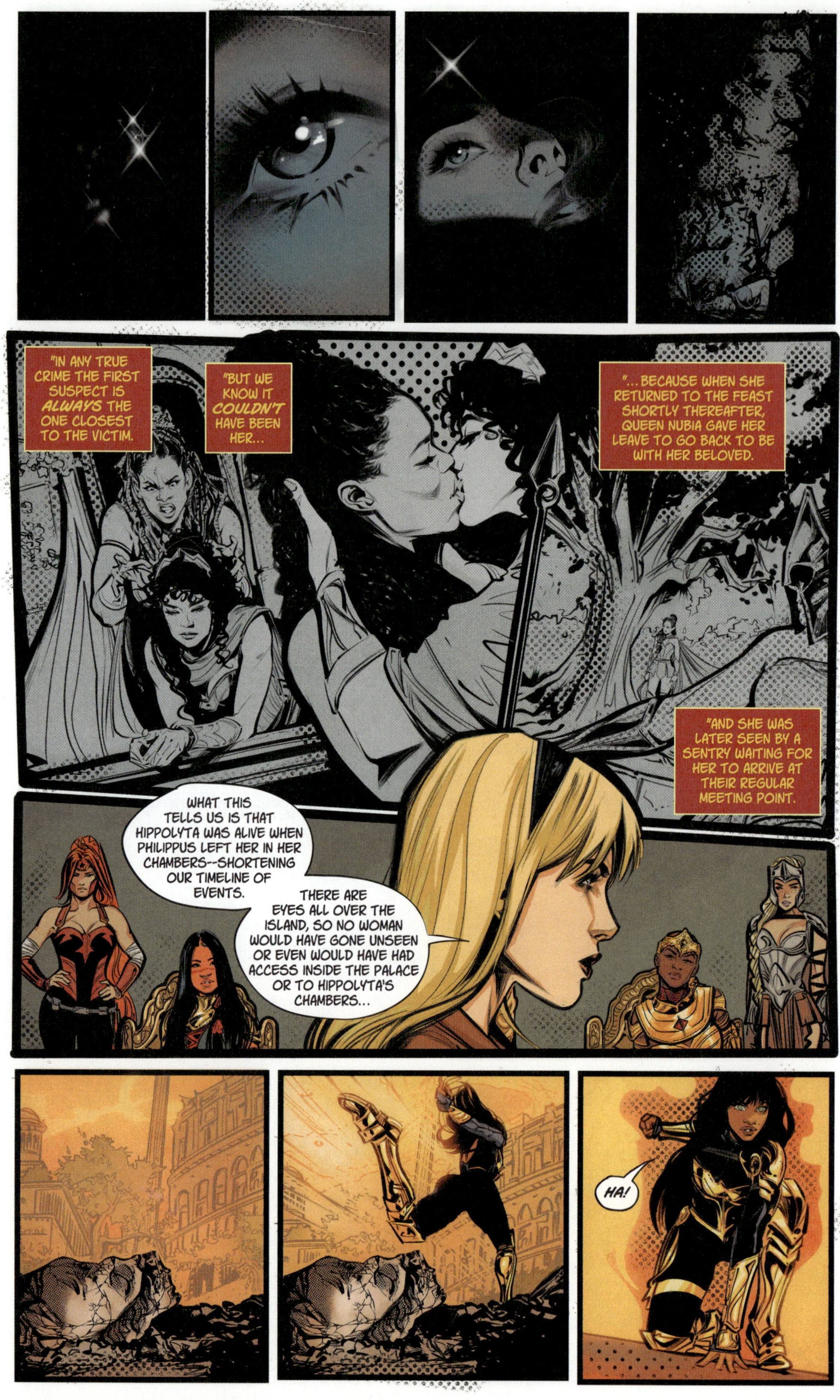
"IN ANY TRUE CRIME THE FIRST SUSPECT IS *ALWAYS* THE ONE CLOSEST TO THE VICTIM.
"BUT WE KNOW IT *COULDN'T* HAVE BEEN HER...
"...BECAUSE WHEN SHE RETURNED TO THE FEAST SHORTLY THEREAFTER, QUEEN NUBIA GAVE HER LEAVE TO GO BACK TO BE WITH HER BELOVED.
"AND SHE WAS LATER SEEN BY A SENTRY WAITING FOR HER TO ARRIVE AT THEIR REGULAR MEETING POINT.
WHAT THIS TELLS US IS THAT HIPPOLYTA WAS ALIVE WHEN PHILIPPUS LEFT HER IN HER CHAMBERS--SHORTENING OUR TIMELINE OF EVENTS.
THERE ARE EYES ALL OVER THE ISLAND, SO NO WOMAN WOULD HAVE GONE UNSEEN OR EVEN WOULD HAVE HAD ACCESS INSIDE THE PALACE OR TO HIPPOLYTA'S CHAMBERS...
HA!

GRRRRRHHH!
"...EXCEPT THOSE REMAINING ON THE DAIS!
THESE WOMEN HAD DIRECT ACCESS TO THE PASSAGEWAYS INSIDE THE PALACE THAT WERE FOR THE MOST PART UNGUARDED. THAT MEANS ANY OF YOU HAD AMPLE OPPORTUNITY!
LET'S START WITH YOU, FARUKA--
ALL RIGHT, LITTLE ONE, LET'S START WITH ME.
"SITTING NEXT TO ATALANTA, YOU TWO SEEMED TO SHARE SOME SECRETS.
"SECRETS THAT SEEMED TO UPSET YOU."
C'MON, YARA!
WE DON'T HAVE TIME FOR YOU TO POSE, WE HAVE TO GET THE NEWS TO QUEEN NUBIA!
FINE! BUT YOU GUYS OWE ME SOME POSE TIME LATER!

CCR-
--AACK--
--CCKK
"...CAUSING AN ALTERCATION BETWEEN YOU AND YARA FLOR."
YES, THAT'S RIGHT, ATALANTA BROUGHT THE POTENTIAL ALTERCATION TO MY ATTENTION, JUST AS I WAS MAKING MOVES TO RETIRE FOR THE EVENING.
I THEN FELT IT NECESSARY TO STAY IN THE HALL IN CASE ANY OTHER SITUATION MIGHT ARISE DURING THE REVELRY. I WAS THE LAST TO LEAVE.
I ALSO NOTICED THAT WHILE SEATED AT THE TABLE, QUEEN FARUKA'S GLASS NEVER SEEMED TO EMPTY. ATALANTA, WERE YOU SO GENEROUS WITH YOUR POUR FOR FARUKA ALONE?
IN INSTIGATING A FIGHT, YOU ENSURED QUEEN NUBIA WOULD FEEL IT NECESSARY TO STAY BEHIND, GIVING THE MURDERER AMPLE TIME TO CARRY OUT THE POISONING. WERE YOU HELPING SOMEONE?!
I WAS MERELY TAKING PART IN THE FESTIVITIES, SAME AS YOU.
WHILE I'D LIKE TO BELIEVE THAT, YOUR ACTIONS THAT NIGHT SEEM VERY QUESTIONABLE. BUT STILL, IT EXCLUDES YOU AS THE KILLER, UNLESS IT IS POSSIBLE FOR YOU TO BE IN TWO PLACES AT ONCE.
THIS LEAVES THE ESQUECIDA IN DOUBT--
HURRY UP!

RAAARGH!
POTIRA!
"YOU HAD THE OPPORTUNITY. IT WOULD HAVE BEEN EASY FOR YOU TO SLIP OUT UNDETECTED DURING THE COMMOTION.
"YOU CERTAINLY HAD THE MEANS...
"...YOUR LOST TRIBE HAS VAST KNOWLEDGE OF POISONS AND THEIR USES.
...OF WHICH I WILL GET INTO FURTHER IN A MOMENT.
GROAN!

BUT WHAT COULD POSSIBLY BE THEIR MOTIVE FOR MURDER?
THEY ARE NOT A WARRING TRIBE LIKE THE BANA-MIGHDALL. THEY DO NOT WISH TO CLAIM ANY THRONE OR HOLD ANY POWER ON THEMYSCIRA. THEY CAME ONLY TO ENSURE THAT THE GUARDIANSHIP AND RESPONSIBILITY FOR **DOOM'S DOORWAY** WAS BEING LOOKED AFTER.
MURDERING ONE OF THE MOST IMPORTANT FIGURES TO THE HOST WOULD ONLY CREATE **CHAOS** AND DISCORD AMONG ALL THREE TRIBES, THREATEN THE BALANCE OF NATURE ITSELF, AND UPSET HER VERY STRONG AND WELL-CONNECTED DAUGHTER.
NOTHING I COULD THINK OF COULD MAKE THAT PUZZLE PIECE FIT.
**SO?!** WHO **MURDERED** HER THEN?!
"I'M GETTING THERE...
"IN MY INVESTIGATION OF HIPPOLYTA'S QUARTERS AFTER HER DEATH, SOMETHING THERE KEPT NAGGING AT ME--MY MIND, OR RATHER MY NOSE, KEPT FOCUSING ON ONE THING. THE ***SMELL!***
"SOMETHING ABOUT THE RESIDUE OF THE POISON LEFT IN THE CHALICE SEEMED SO ***FAMILIAR...***

COUGH
"ONCE MIXED IT BECOMES TASTELESS AND CARRIES THE SLIGHTEST SMELL OF SPICED HONEY THAT WOULD ONLY COMPLIMENT THE EARTHY AROMA OF THE WINE. BUT ONCE INGESTED...
"THAT SOMETHING MADE THE ESQUECIDA IMMEDIATELY SUSPECT. WHILE I SEARCHED FOR YARA FLOR DEEP IN THE JUNGLES OF BRAZIL I FOUND MYSELF HYPNOTIZED BY A SWEET AND ALMOST TANGY SMELL THAT WOULD OCCASIONALLY DRIFT THROUGH THE AIR.
"I WAS QUICKLY WARNED NEVER TO FOLLOW IT, FOR IT CAME FROM A SACRED TREE THAT PRODUCES SAP AS POISONOUS AS ITS SCENT WAS ENCHANTING.
"EVEN THE SMALLEST AMOUNT WILL CAUSE THE MUSCLES IN THE THROAT TO CLENCH TIGHTER THAN THE FINAL CONSTRICTION OF A SNAKE, CUTTING OFF ALL ACCESS TO OXYGEN, THUS STRANGLING THE VICTIM TO DEATH."

COUGH
COUGH COUGH
WHERE?
BUT IT WASN'T ONLY YOU I GAVE THE WARNING TO--
"PRECISELY!
"THIS SAME PERSON WAS ALSO MISSING FROM THE DAIS AT JUST THE RIGHT TIME--
"THE VERY PERSON WITH ME IN BRAZIL WHO LEARNED ABOUT THE SAME POISON USED TO KILL HIPPOLYTA!
CRACK

OF ALL THE PLACES!
HA!
HA HA!
HA HA HA!
IT COULD ONLY HAVE BEEN ONE PERSON...
...ARTEMIS!
GUARDS!
RESTRAIN HER!
SOME SAY POISON IS A COWARD'S WEAPON. I THINK THAT'S ONE WAY OF LOOKING AT IT, BUT PUT THIS WEAPON IN THE HANDS OF ONE OF THE GREATEST WARRIORS KNOWN TO ALL AMAZONS...

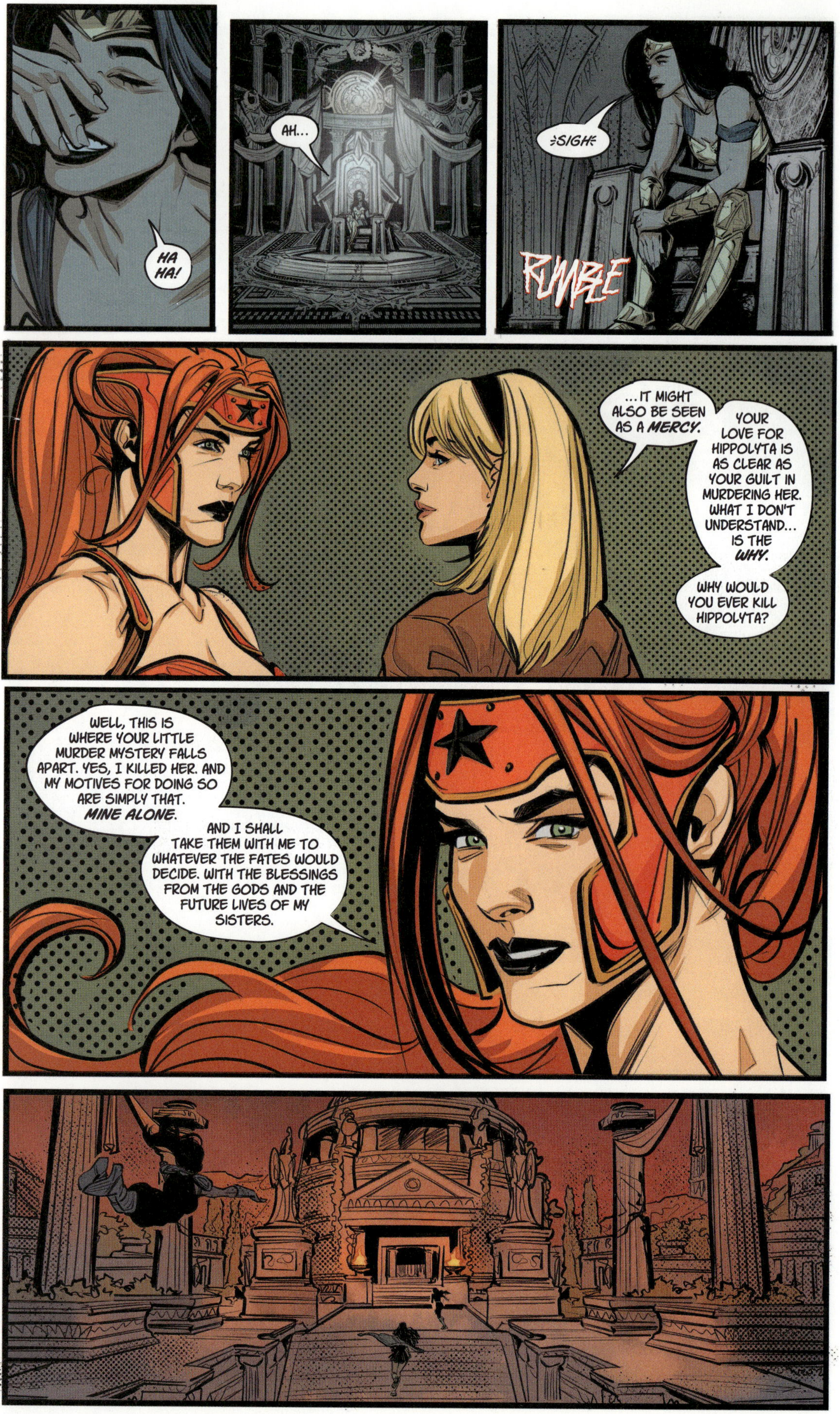
HA HA!
AH...
SIGH
RUMBLE
...IT MIGHT ALSO BE SEEN AS A *MERCY*.
YOUR LOVE FOR HIPPOLYTA IS AS CLEAR AS YOUR GUILT IN MURDERING HER. WHAT I DON'T UNDERSTAND... IS THE *WHY*.
WHY WOULD YOU EVER KILL HIPPOLYTA?
WELL, THIS IS WHERE YOUR LITTLE MURDER MYSTERY FALLS APART. YES, I KILLED HER. AND MY MOTIVES FOR DOING SO ARE SIMPLY THAT. *MINE ALONE*.
AND I SHALL TAKE THEM WITH ME TO WHATEVER THE FATES WOULD DECIDE. WITH THE BLESSINGS FROM THE GODS AND THE FUTURE LIVES OF MY SISTERS.

?
CRASK
RUMBLE
SECURE HER IN THE SENATE ANTEROOM AND PREPARE HER FOR THE JOURNEY TO REFORM ISLAND...
...FOR SHE NOT ONLY MURDERED A MOTHER TO ALL AMAZONS AND OUR FORMER QUEEN...
...BUT ALSO MY HEART. TAKE HER AWAY.
RUMBLE
RUMBLE
WHAT'S THIS?!
UH... GUYS? WHAT'S HAPPENING? THE PALACE...

AN EARTHQUAKE?!
WHAM
HOW ON EARTH DID I GET HERE BEFORE YOU THREE?!

MY QUEEN! THE PALACE, IT IS FALLING!

THE PALACE! IT IS DESTROYED!
WHAT IS THE CAUSE OF THIS?
LOOK! SOMETHING IS RISING IN ITS PLACE!

RUMBLE RUMBLE
DOOM'S DOORWAY?!
TRIAL OF THE AMAZONS PART 6
JOËLLE JONES SCRIPT JOËLLE JONES AND ADRIANA MELO ART JORDIE BELLAIRE COLORS PAT BROSSEAU LETTERS
JONES AND BELLAIRE COVER BABS TARR VARIANT COVER JILLIAN GRANT ASSISTANT EDITOR BRITTANY HOLZHERR EDITOR
PAUL KAMINSKI GROUP EDITOR WONDER WOMAN CREATED BY WILLIAM MOULTON MARSTON

*Trial of the Amazons* #2 cover by Jim Cheung and Jay David Ramos

Trial of the Amazons #2 variant cover by Rose Besch

CHAOS.
FIRST OF THE PRIMORDIAL GODS.
THEMYSCIRA.
WHY IS HE DOING THIS? WHAT DOES HE WANT?
DOES IT MATTER? WE MUST STOP HIM!
NO!
YOU WILL ALL STAND DOWN!
I WAS THE ONE WHO IMPRISONED CHAOS IN THE GRAVEYARD OF THE GODS. IT'S ME HE'S AFTER.*
I WON'T LET ANY MORE OF MY SISTERS DIE FOR MY MISTAKE! LEAVE, EVACUATE THE ISLAND. SAVE AS MANY AS YOU CAN!
SKISH
*SEE WONDER WOMAN #775! -- BRITTANY
YEAH, RIGHT! PACK IT UP WHILE MY PEOPLE ARE IN TROUBLE?
I'M AN AMAZON, JUST LIKE YOU. THAT MEANS I'M GONNA FIGHT.
YARA...!
SHE'S RIGHT, DIANA.

WE'RE ALL AMAZONS. THAT MEANS WE FIGHT TOGETHER.
TRIAL OF THE AMAZONS FINALE
BECKY CLOONAN, MICHAEL W. CONRAD, VITA AYALA, STEPHANIE WILLIAMS AND JOËLLE JONES SCRIPT
ELENA CASAGRANDE, LAURA BRAGA, SKYLAR PATRIDGE, ADRIANA MELO AND JOËLLE JONES ARTISTS
ROMULO FAJARDO JR. AND JORDIE BELLAIRE COLORISTS PAT BROSSEAU LETTERER JIM CHEUNG AND
JAY DAVID RAMOS COVER ROSE BESCH VARIANT COVER CHRIS ROSA ASSOCIATE EDITOR BRITTANY HOLZHERR EDITOR
PAUL KAMINSKI GROUP EDITOR WONDER WOMAN CREATED BY WILLIAM MOULTON MARSTON

TOGETHER, THEN.

Diana! You left me to rot, to molder among the dead.
What hubris to believe Chaos itself could be entombed!
I NEVER FORGOT MY OATH! I WOULD HAVE RETURNED AND FOUND A WAY TO RELEASE YOU!
WHOOSH
Yet here I stand, desecrating the hallowed soil of your isle!
Let us see which of us will cheat the grave one last time.
ENOUGH BLOOD HAS BEEN SPILLED!
GO! RETURN TO OLYMPUS. EVEN AFTER WHAT YOU'VE DONE, I WILL SEE THAT YOU ARE TREATED FAIRLY!
HNNGH ALL ARE DUE THE CHANCE OF REDEMPTION.
Ha ha ha!
How orderly of you, Diana...and how naive. I am older than philosophy, older than the turning of the planets.
I am the Apeiron, boundless discord! And you...you are a bug.
"All are due redemption." Ha! Even Artemis?
Your mother's killer? You would see her redeemed?
GET OUT OF MY HEAD!

TAPPING OUT ALREADY?
UNGH!
THUDD
FARUKA... I FELT MY HOLD SLIP, BUT I'M NOT ABOUT TO GIVE UP.
STEEL YOUR MINDS. WE MUSTN'T LET CHAOS IN.
HE IS THE SOURCE OF THE STRIFE THAT HAS BEFALLEN OUR TRIBES. HE'LL TEAR US APART IF WE GIVE HIM THE POWER.
THE GHOST...
I SEE IT TOO!
OLD THOUGH I MAY BE, I'M NO GHOST YET.
SHING
ANTIOPE!
BEFORE, IN THE TEMPLE... THAT WAS YOU?
YOU WERE WISE TO HEED MY WORDS-- THEY WERE YOUR MOTHER'S.
THIS IS NOT HOW WE MEANT IT TO BE, BUT YOU CANNOT STOP THE WHEEL OF FATE FROM TURNING.
IF YOU DARE TO FIGHT A GOD...

"...YOU WILL REQUIRE WEAPONS FORGED BY THE GODS THEMSELVES."
MAGALA! LOOK! THE SENATE BUILDING IS STILL STANDING!
HURRY! WE DON'T HAVE LONG!
QUEEN NUBIA, WE MUST GET TO THE ARMORY!
BUT THE ARMORY IS NO MORE.
THERE IS ANOTHER!
THIS WAY!

I'M SORRY, QUEEN. I NEVER HAD THE OPPORTUNITY TO TELL YOU ABOUT THIS PLACE.
CLICK
CREAK
SWOOSH
SHUNK
SWEET!
COME ON. FOR CENTURIES, THIS IS WHERE WE'VE KEPT OUR MOST SACRED AMAZONIAN WEAPONS AND ARTIFACTS.

MOST OF WHAT IS KEPT HERE ARE ITEMS WE HOPED TO LEAVE UNTOUCHED. BUT WHAT IS AN AMAZON IF NOT SOMEONE WHO IS ALWAYS PREPARED FOR VICTORY?
WELCOME TO THE WAR CHEST OF NIKE.
I LOVE BEING AN AMAZON!
I NEED TO VISIT MORE OFTEN. I'VE CLEARLY BEEN MISSING OUT!
BLESS!

WHAT A GORGEOUSLY CRAFTED PIECE.
AN IMPORTANT PART OF AMAZON HISTORY. THAT IS ARMOR WORN BY A PAST CHAMPION, ASTERIA. SHE HELD BACK HORDES OF MALE WARRIORS WHILE WEARING IT.
IS THAT A PLANE?
DIANA'S INVISIBLE JET. YOU ARE ALSO HOLDING THE SWORD OF ATHENA.
WHOA!
WHERE DID CASSIE GO?
SHE MENTIONED GETTING SOMETHING WE'LL NEED FROM ANOTHER ROOM.
I KNOW THEY'RE KEEPING HER SOMEWHERE IN HERE.
AH, THIS MUST BE IT!
WE NEED YOU...

...ARTEMIS!
HOW DID YOU FIND ME?
I'M A DETECTIVE, REMEMBER?
WHAT THE HELL IS GOING ON OUT THERE?
PURE CHAOS. LET'S GET OUT OF HERE WHILE WE STILL CAN.
THIS IS COMPLETELY UNNECESSARY. I COULD'VE RUN.
SURE, BUT FLYING IS ALWAYS FASTER.
WHY WOULD YOU LET HER OUT?
OUR BEST CHANCE AT BEATING WHAT WE'RE UP AGAINST REQUIRES OUR BEST.
CASSIE IS RIGHT.
ALL AMAZONS ON DECK!

On the Battlefield.
WE CAN'T KEEP THIS UP FOREVER!
CERTAINLY NOT, IF THE DOORWAY SPEWING MONSTERS HAS ANYTHING TO SAY ABOUT IT.
THE DOORWAY IS THE ROOT OF THIS--WE HAVE TO STEM THE FLOW!
HIYAH!
THEN TO THE SOURCE OF THIS MESS!
WHAK
AMAZONS, FOLLOW ME!
I'M SORRY, SISTER.
ABOUT TIME YOU DECIDED TO JOIN THE FRAY.
WE THOUGHT WE'D ADDRESS THE ORIGIN OF THE PROBLEM, INSTEAD OF FIGHTING AMONG OURSELVES.
I--
LATER, GENERAL.
NOW IS NOT FOR SPEAKING, BUT FOR FIGHTING.

AND REMEMBER, WE DO NOT KILL OUR OWN!

AVOID THE OIL OF CHAOS, SISTERS!
LET NOT THE ENEMY MAKE YOU A WEAPON AGAINST EACH OTHER!

PLEASE, SISTER, CENTER YOUR MIND AND GAIN CONTROL OF YOUR EMOTIONS.
I MORE THAN MOST KNOW HOW SEDUCTIVE THE SONG OF CHAOS IS, BUT IT CAN BE OVERCOME. YOU *MUST* BE STRONG AND SURE IN YOURSELF!
YARRRRGGGHH!
NICE TRICK.
THAT WILL PROVE USEFUL.
UGH!
TANGGG
IT WAS AN HONOR TO FIGHT BY YOUR SIDE, SISTER.
THE HONOR WAS MINE, MY QUEEN.
WHOOSH

WHIP WHIP WHIP WHIP
I--IS SHE--?
SHE LIVES AND WILL REGAIN HER MIND.
IT WOULD HAVE SERVED YOU BETTER TO LET US DIE.
WE ARE SISTERS, FARUKA, NONE BETTER THAN THE OTHER.
ALL WILL FIGHT AND DIE FOR EACH OTHER.
ALL WILL FIGHT TO SAVE EACH OTHER.
HMM.
PANT PANT PANT
UP. GET UP, ARTEMIS...
...THERE IS STILL WORK TO DO.
ATALANTA AND ANTIOPE GATHER THEIR FORCES AT THE DOOR, AND CHAOS FOLLOWS!

CHAOS! IN THE NAME OF APEIRON, WE INVOKE YOU! HEAR OUR PRAYER!
GIVE US YOUR BLESSING, O LORD OF BEDLAM!
Ha ha ha! You openly accept my power? Very well...
Take the gifts of entropy!
GLADLY. WE RECEIVE YOUR ESSENCE...
ALL OF IT.
No...no! What are you doing?!
One by one, every Amazon will fall!
I shall take you all down with me--
I refuse to be interred again!
I will not-- Urraggh!
ANTIOPE! ATALANTA, NO! CHAOS WILL DESTROY YOU!
SOMEONE, STOP THEM!
HUSH, DIANA. LONG HAVE WE KNOWN OUR FATE WOULD BE ONE OF SACRIFICE.
WITH THIS KNOWLEDGE CAME PEACE, AND THE STRENGTH OF UNIFIED AMAZONS.
WE CAN HOLD HIM, BUT ONLY FOR A TIME... AND THAT TIME IS LIMITED.
Aaaauughh...
TRUST US, DIANA. AS YOU ALWAYS HAVE.
WE SUBMIT OURSELVES, FOR OUR SISTERS.

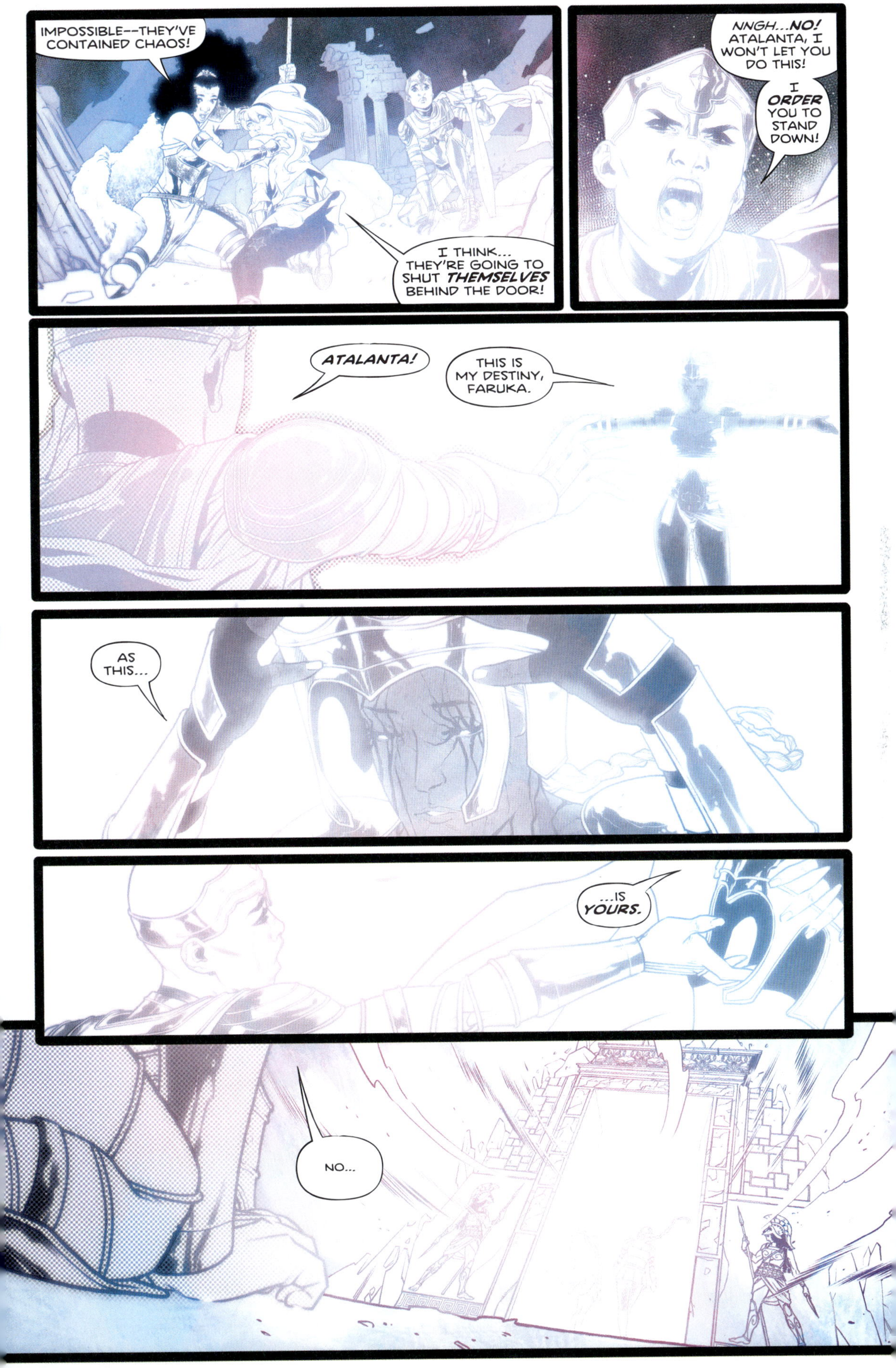
IMPOSSIBLE--THEY'VE CONTAINED CHAOS!
I THINK... THEY'RE GOING TO SHUT THEMSELVES BEHIND THE DOOR!
NNGH...NO! ATALANTA, I WON'T LET YOU DO THIS!
I ORDER YOU TO STAND DOWN!
ATALANTA!
THIS IS MY DESTINY, FARUKA.
AS THIS...
...IS YOURS.
NO...

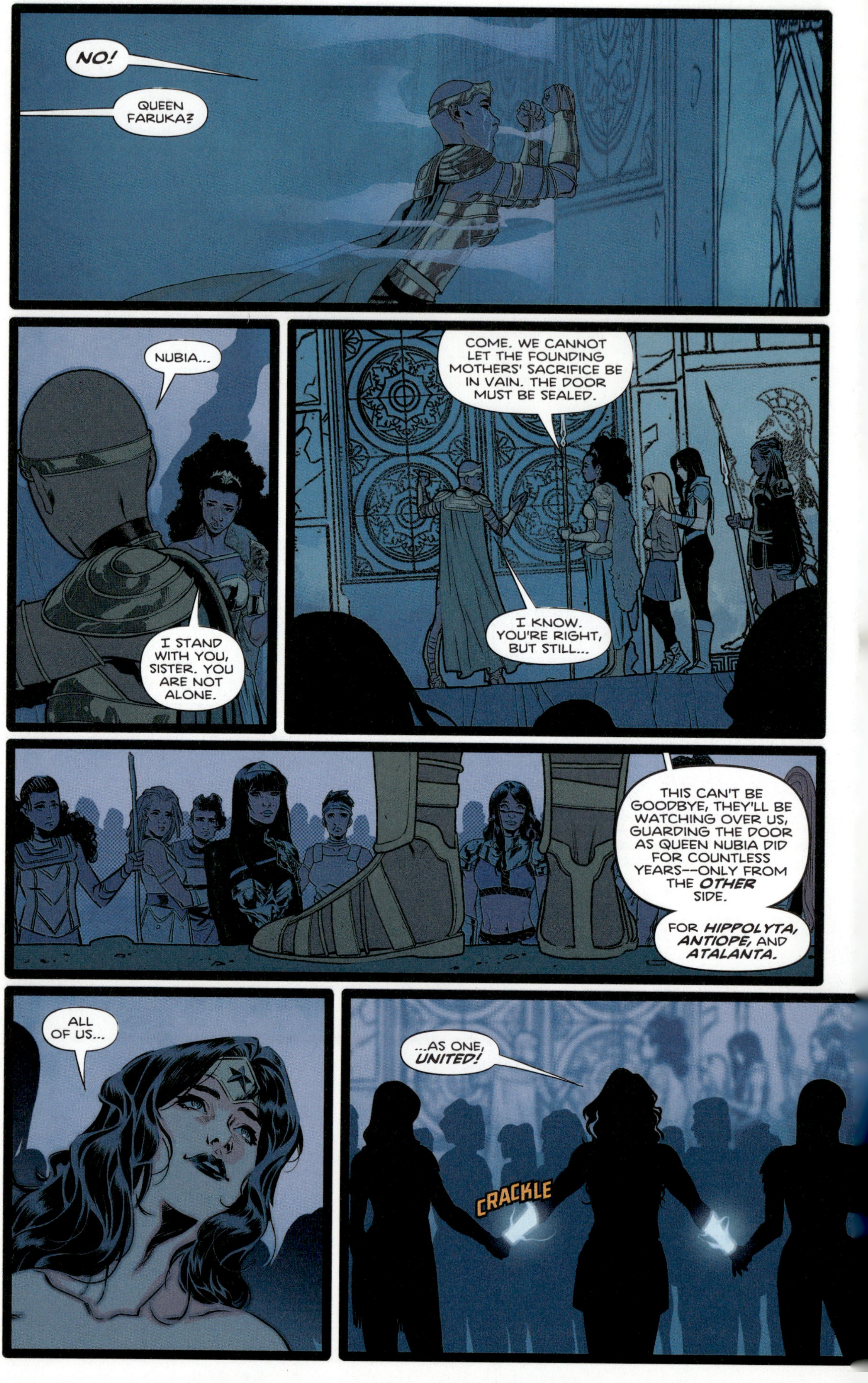
NO!
QUEEN FARUKA?
NUBIA...
I STAND WITH YOU, SISTER. YOU ARE NOT ALONE.
COME. WE CANNOT LET THE FOUNDING MOTHERS' SACRIFICE BE IN VAIN. THE DOOR MUST BE SEALED.
I KNOW. YOU'RE RIGHT, BUT STILL...
THIS CAN'T BE GOODBYE, THEY'LL BE WATCHING OVER US, GUARDING THE DOOR AS QUEEN NUBIA DID FOR COUNTLESS YEARS--ONLY FROM THE *OTHER* SIDE.
FOR *HIPPOLYTA, ANTIOPE,* AND *ATALANTA.*
ALL OF US...
...AS ONE, *UNITED!*
CRACKLE

THE DOOR...BY THE GRACE OF HATHOR, IT SEALED ITSELF!
THIS WAS NO MIRACLE...
SHAAAA --
-- SHOOOOM!
HECATE'S FLAME, THAT WAS MAGIC.
PRESERVE US. FORGIVE US. WE SHALL ALWAYS HONOR YOUR SACRIFICES.

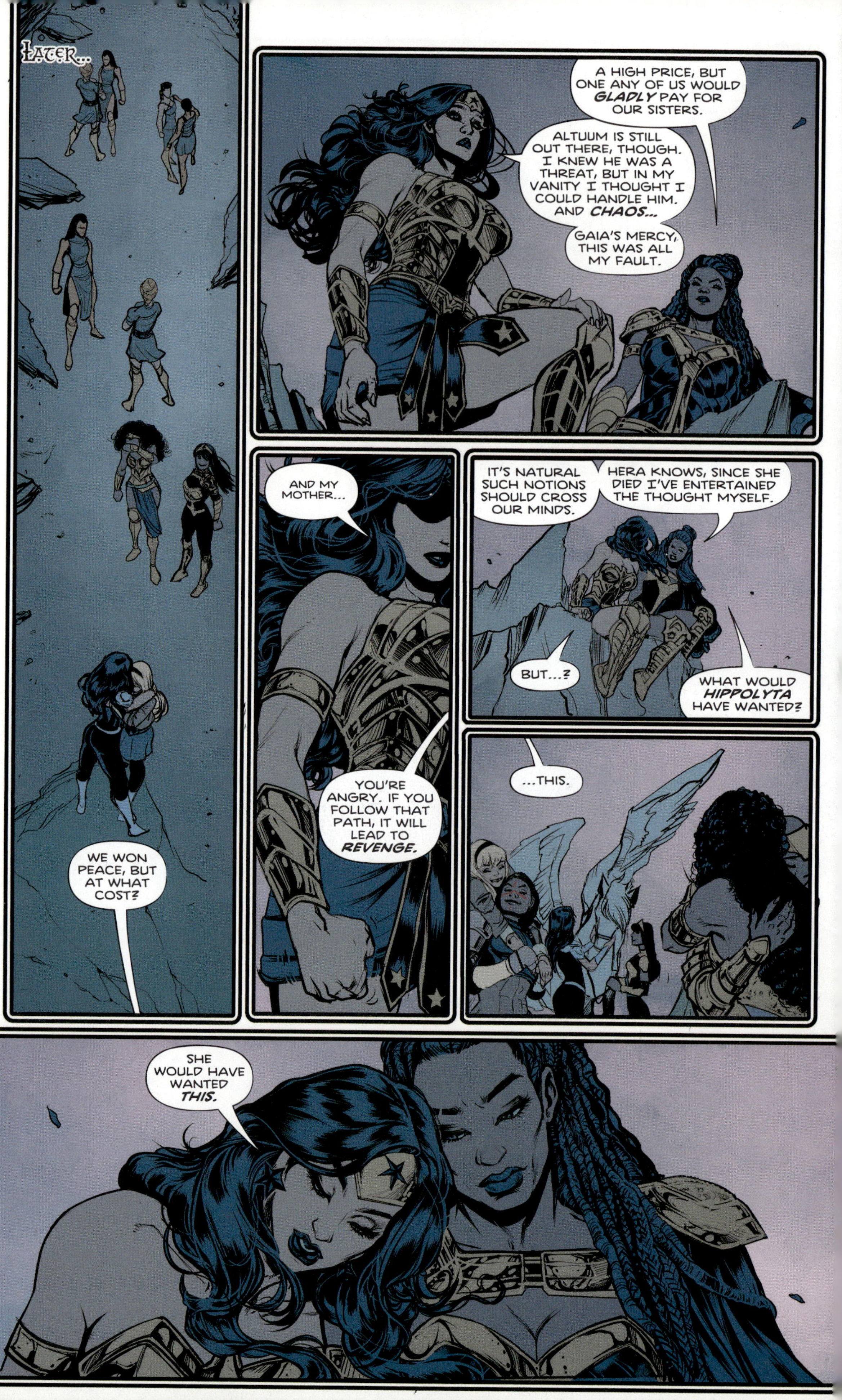
LATER...
WE WON PEACE, BUT AT WHAT COST?
A HIGH PRICE, BUT ONE ANY OF US WOULD *GLADLY* PAY FOR OUR SISTERS.
ALTUUM IS STILL OUT THERE, THOUGH. I KNEW HE WAS A THREAT, BUT IN MY VANITY I THOUGHT I COULD HANDLE HIM. AND *CHAOS...*
GAIA'S MERCY, THIS WAS ALL MY FAULT.
AND MY MOTHER...
YOU'RE ANGRY. IF YOU FOLLOW THAT PATH, IT WILL LEAD TO *REVENGE.*
IT'S NATURAL SUCH NOTIONS SHOULD CROSS OUR MINDS.
HERA KNOWS, SINCE SHE DIED I'VE ENTERTAINED THE THOUGHT MYSELF.
BUT...?
WHAT WOULD *HIPPOLYTA* HAVE WANTED?
...THIS.
SHE WOULD HAVE WANTED *THIS.*

NIGHT HAS FULLY SET IN OVER THE ISLAND OF THEMYSCIRA ONCE MORE.
IN ITS STATE OF POST-TRAUMA, LIFE BEGINS AGAIN. ALL LEND THEIR HANDS TO THE TASKS OF REBUILDING, AND SEEDS OF FAMILIAL LOVE BEGIN TO TAKE ROOT BETWEEN THE MEMBERS OF THE THREE TRIBES...
...HINTING AT A POSSIBLE ARMISTICE FOR FUTURE PEACE... POSSIBLY.
BUT BEFORE BEST-LAID PLANS HAVE ANY CHANCE OF GOING AWRY, ONE LAST TASK NEEDS COMPLETING THIS NIGHT.
YARA?
YEAH?
CAN YOU COME WITH ME? I WOULD LIKE TO SHOW YOU SOMETHING.

SOMEWHERE DEEP BELOW THE ARMORY.
WHAT IS IT?
JUST WAIT...
WELCOME TO THE *TIAR-MORY!**
*NAME COURTESY OF THE ONE AND ONLY BECKY CLOONAN. --JOËLLE
WELL, AT LEAST THAT'S WHAT I CALL IT. A COLLECTION OF PRECIOUS, SOMETIMES SACRED, SIGNIFIERS.
BAUBLES USED AS ORNAMENT, SOMETIMES WEAPON, BUT ALSO A TRADITION.
EACH ONE SEEMINGLY SMALL AND SIMPLE, YET EACH WITH THEIR OWN BURDEN OF SIGNIFICANCE.
I NOTICE YOU WEAR ONE OF YOUR OWN...

OH... IT'S NOT...
IT WAS GIFTED TO YOU BY THE GODDESS HERA, WAS IT NOT?
IT WAS, BUT I...
I KNOW YOU CARE NOT FOR OUR GODS.
SNAP
HEY! WHOA!
YOU REMIND ME OF PROMETHEUS...
IT REALLY TIED THE WHOLE ENSEMBLE TOGETHER--
YOU STOLE A FLAME FROM OLYMPUS, BUT IT WAS A FIRE OF YOUR OWN MAKING YOU TOOK.
...AND IN SHARING THAT INNER FIRE, YOU CONVINCED US TO ABANDON OUR DIVINE TRADITIONS...
...AND TO INSTEAD FOLLOW OUR MORTAL QUALITIES OF COURAGE, CUNNING, AND STRENGTH TO WIN THE DAY.
YOU DID ALL THIS IN THE FACE OF ADVERSITY SO THAT WE MAY FURTHER A MISSION TO MAKE THE WORLD SAFE FOR ALL, GOD AND MORTAL ALIKE, TO FLOURISH.
SO...

...I ASK YOU NOW TO KNEEL, YARA FLOR.
IT IS BECAUSE OF THIS, I GIFT TO YOU A MORE FITTING CROWN, ESCHEWING YOUR PREVIOUSLY GIVEN SINGLE STAR FOR THREE, THREE STARS FOR THREE TRIBES, *NOW UNIFIED!*
AND TO NOW BE KNOWN TO THE WORLD AS...
...WONDER GIRL!
*WONDER-GIRL? GIRL?* YOU KNOW I'M IN MY TWENTIES, RIGHT?
NO, I KNOW, IT IS MEANT TO BE--
IT'S JUST A LITTLE INSULTING TO BE CALLED A GIRL...

WELL, SYMBOLISM ASIDE, WHEN YOU HAVE LIVED AS LONG AS I HAVE--
I'M NOT SAYING I DON'T APPRECIATE--
THE TITLE *GIRL*--
IT'S JUST LIKE, ***WOW!*** REALLY?--
YOU HAVE TO UNDERSTAND--
SEEMS LIKE YOU WOULD HAVE YOUR HANDS FULL WITH TWO WONDER GIRLS ALREADY--
WELL CASSIE AND DONNA--
IS THIS A BATMAN THING, LIKE WITH THE ROBINS? SHOULD I BE WORRIED?
*SIGH* WHAT? NO--
*--BUT--*
...BUT?
BUT, ***THANK YOU,*** I MEAN IT, TRULY.
YOU ARE A VERY DIFFERENT GIRL THAN I AM USED TO, YARA, BUT I THINK IT COULD BE A GOOD THING.
WOMAN. A VERY DIFFERENT ***WOMAN.***
YES, YES YOU ARE!

THE RESTORED HALL OF CELEBRATION, THE PALACE OF THEMYSCIRA.
MANY, MANY DAYS LATER.
DRINK, SISTER, WE HAVE WORKED LONG AND HARD THIS DAY.
AHEM.
IF I MAY HAVE YOUR EARS?
BEFORE ME SIT THEMYSCIRAN, BANA-MIGHDALL, AND ESQUECIDA... SISTERS, ALL.
TOGETHER WE HAVE FACED TRAGEDY, AND TOGETHER WE HAVE GROWN TO BE ONE PEOPLE.
MY HEART IS HEAVY FOR WHAT WE HAVE LOST, BUT I STAND HERE, PROUD TO BE AMONG YOUR NUMBER.

"I WILL ADMIT, I AM NOT ONE FOR SPEECHES.
"IT ISN'T A LACK OF PATIENCE-- AS FORMER CHAMPION OF THE DOORWAY, I LEARNED THE VIRTUE OF RESTRAINT AND ENDURANCE.
"BUT I BELIEVE THAT IT IS ONE'S ACTIONS, NOT THEIR WORDS, THAT HOLD THEIR TRUTH.
BEYOND YOUR SWORDS, EVERY SINGLE ONE OF YOU HAS GIVEN OF YOUR STRENGTH AND SPIRIT TO HELP REBUILD SOME OF WHAT WAS LOST HERE.
YOUR GENEROSITY AND KINDNESS, YOUR DRIVE TO RAISE UP YOUR SISTERS, IS HUMBLING AND INSPIRING.
THERE IS NO WAY TO PROPERLY EXPRESS THE LOVE I FEEL WHEN LOOKING AT ALL OF YOU. INSTEAD, I WILL SPEND THE REST OF MY DAYS ***WORKING TO BE WORTHY*** TO SHARE THE NAME OF ***AMAZON*** WITH YOU ALL.
*COUGH COUGH*

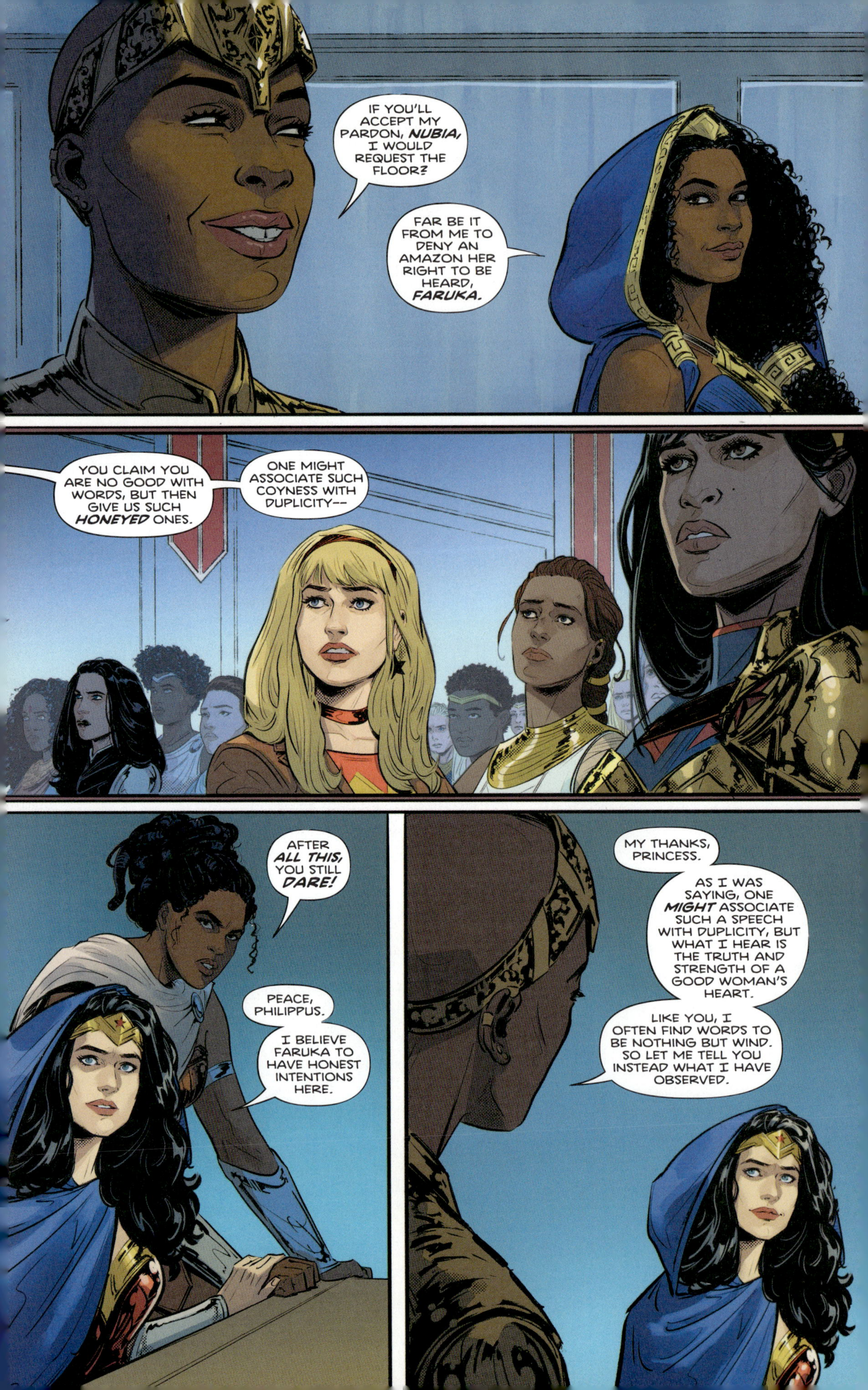
IF YOU'LL ACCEPT MY PARDON, NUBIA, I WOULD REQUEST THE FLOOR?
FAR BE IT FROM ME TO DENY AN AMAZON HER RIGHT TO BE HEARD, FARUKA.
YOU CLAIM YOU ARE NO GOOD WITH WORDS, BUT THEN GIVE US SUCH HONEYED ONES.
ONE MIGHT ASSOCIATE SUCH COYNESS WITH DUPLICITY--
AFTER ALL THIS, YOU STILL DARE!
PEACE, PHILIPPUS.
I BELIEVE FARUKA TO HAVE HONEST INTENTIONS HERE.
MY THANKS, PRINCESS.
AS I WAS SAYING, ONE MIGHT ASSOCIATE SUCH A SPEECH WITH DUPLICITY, BUT WHAT I HEAR IS THE TRUTH AND STRENGTH OF A GOOD WOMAN'S HEART.
LIKE YOU, I OFTEN FIND WORDS TO BE NOTHING BUT WIND. SO LET ME TELL YOU INSTEAD WHAT I HAVE OBSERVED.

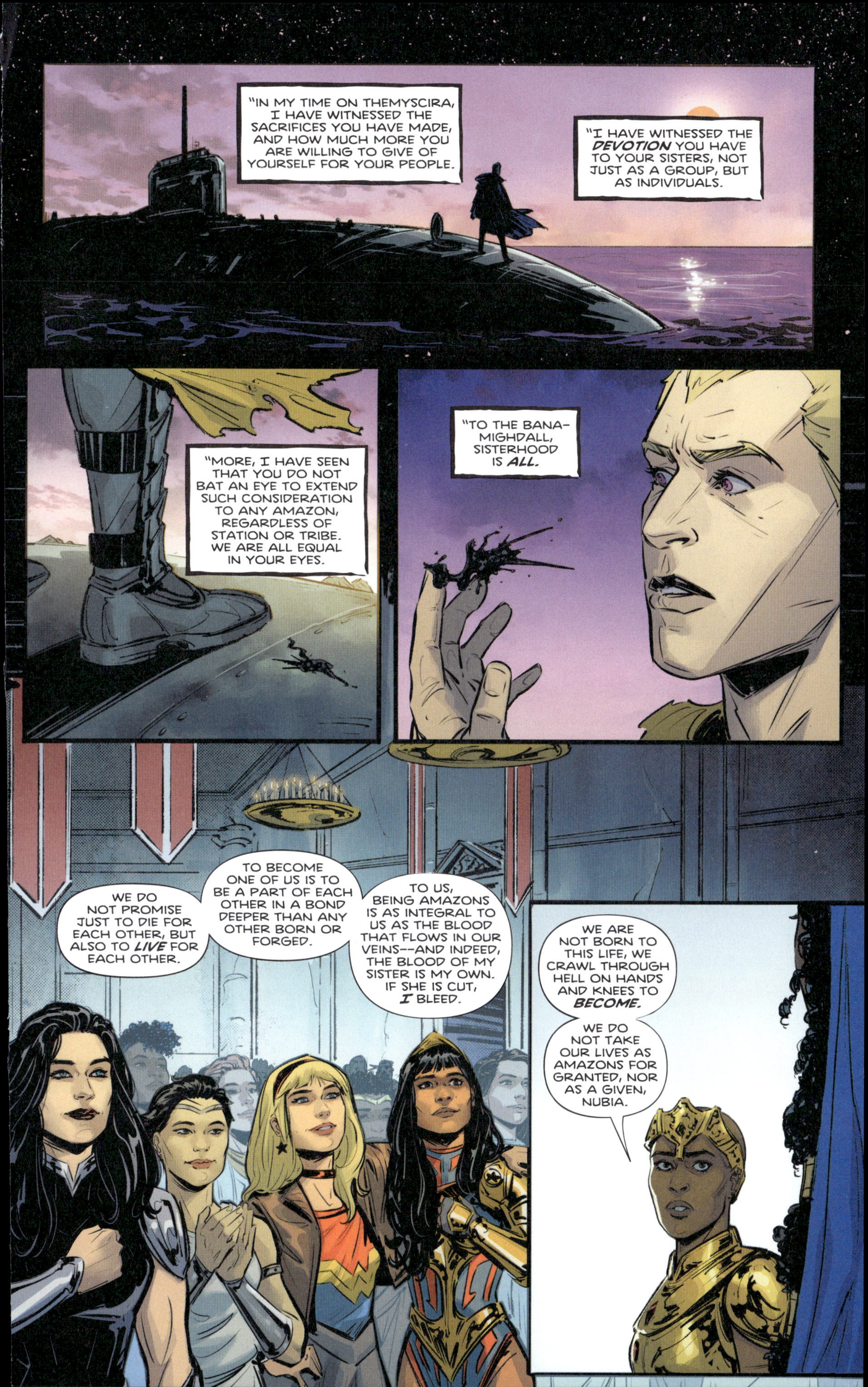
"IN MY TIME ON THEMYSCIRA, I HAVE WITNESSED THE SACRIFICES YOU HAVE MADE, AND HOW MUCH MORE YOU ARE WILLING TO GIVE OF YOURSELF FOR YOUR PEOPLE.
"I HAVE WITNESSED THE DEVOTION YOU HAVE TO YOUR SISTERS, NOT JUST AS A GROUP, BUT AS INDIVIDUALS.
"MORE, I HAVE SEEN THAT YOU DO NOT BAT AN EYE TO EXTEND SUCH CONSIDERATION TO ANY AMAZON, REGARDLESS OF STATION OR TRIBE. WE ARE ALL EQUAL IN YOUR EYES.
"TO THE BANA-MIGHDALL, SISTERHOOD IS ALL.
WE DO NOT PROMISE JUST TO DIE FOR EACH OTHER, BUT ALSO TO LIVE FOR EACH OTHER.
TO BECOME ONE OF US IS TO BE A PART OF EACH OTHER IN A BOND DEEPER THAN ANY OTHER BORN OR FORGED.
TO US, BEING AMAZONS IS AS INTEGRAL TO US AS THE BLOOD THAT FLOWS IN OUR VEINS--AND INDEED, THE BLOOD OF MY SISTER IS MY OWN. IF SHE IS CUT, I BLEED.
WE ARE NOT BORN TO THIS LIFE, WE CRAWL THROUGH HELL ON HANDS AND KNEES TO BECOME.
WE DO NOT TAKE OUR LIVES AS AMAZONS FOR GRANTED, NOR AS A GIVEN, NUBIA.

THIS IS THE CROWN OF ATALANTA, WORN BY ONE OF THE GREATEST WARRIOR QUEENS THIS WORLD HAS EVER KNOWN.
IT IS A SYMBOL OF LEADERSHIP OF THE BANA-MIGHDALL. IT IS EARNED, THROUGH VALOR AND SISTERHOOD AND LOVE.
IT BELONGS TO YOU.
YOU ARE WRONG, FARUKA.
THE HONOR AND RESPECT YOU GIVE ME IS A GIFT.
AND IT IS MY DUTY TO SPEND THE REST OF MY DAYS ATTEMPTING TO BE WORTHY OF IT.
RISE, SISTER, AND I DEEPLY HOPE FRIEND.
TO CALL YOU A FRIEND WOULD BE AN HONOR ENTIRELY ALL MINE, MY QUEEN.
LONG LIVE QUEEN NUBIA!
LONG LIVE THE QUEEN!
LONG LIVE THE QUEEN!
TO BE CONTINUED IN NUBIA: CORONATION SPECIAL #1!

# TRIAL OF THE AMAZONS

VARIANT COVERS

Trial of the Amazons #1 variant cover by Jen Bartel

JEN
BAR
TEL

*Trial of the Amazons* #1 variant cover by Rafael Albuquerque

*Trial of the Amazons* #1 variant cover by Tiago da Silva

*Nubia & the Amazons* #6 International Women's Day variant cover by Juliet Nneka

*Wonder Woman* #785 International Women's Day variant cover by Nicola Scott and Annette Kwok

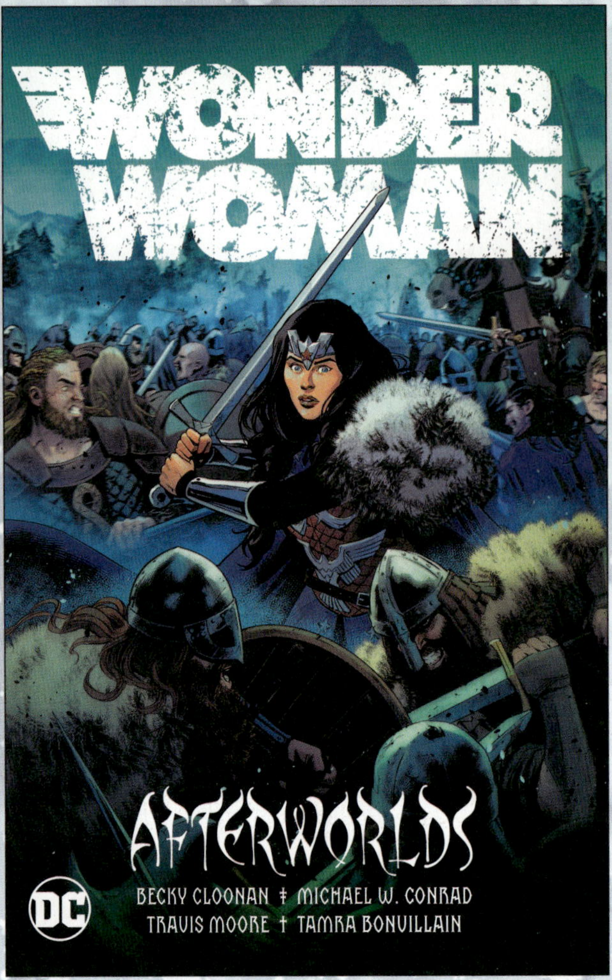


*"The most exciting Diana story in a decade."*
*—AIPT*

# WONDER WOMAN VOL. 1:

**AFTERWORLDS**

BECKY CLOONAN
MICHAEL W. CONRAD
TRAVIS MOORE

**FUTURE STATE: WONDER WOMAN**

**NUBIA & THE AMAZONS**

**WONDER WOMAN BLACK & GOLD**

**GET MORE DC GRAPHIC NOVELS**
WHEREVER COMICS AND BOOKS ARE SOLD!